Change of Heart
The Sweetbriar Mountain Series

Nora Everly

Chapter 1
Cade

I blinked against the silvered glare of the sun on the snow packed road, yawning as I drove. Twelve-hour shifts sucked but working one overnight was the worst. I was exhausted, hungry, and ready to get into bed with the leftover pizza in my fridge and my Netflix account before crashing into a comatose oblivion. I stretched in my seat and continued up the highway into the mountains. Sweetbriar, Oregon, was one of the small towns you'd pass through on your way to Mount Hood. My house was located up in the foothills overlooking town. And thankfully, I was almost there.

"Slow down, damn it," I muttered as a Range Rover passed me, hitting a hidden patch of black ice and fishtailing side to side before regaining control. The out-of-state plates let me know how clueless they were about the danger they were in. Plus, what kind of dumbass passes a cop?

My head whipped to the side as a Subaru sped

around me, driving right up to the bumper of the Range Rover. "What the hell?"

I switched my lights and siren on, hoping it would suffice as a warning as it was too slick for a pursuit. It was ski season, and the roads were full of vacationers with no clue how to drive in the snow. I couldn't put the other vehicles at risk by chasing these two boneheads down. On a day like this, just being out on the roads was hazardous enough. A police chase between three cars would wreak more havoc than letting them go. But I called it in to the station so everyone would be on the lookout and hoped I wouldn't come across their mangled wreckage further up the highway.

I was not in the mood for that kind of paperwork.

All I had wanted was to go home, have a snack, and crash. But I had an ominous feeling that wasn't going to happen. The crackle of my radio interrupted my thoughts and I cursed.

The voice of the dispatcher on duty asked, "Cade, do you copy?"

"Yeah, unfortunately."

"I'm sorry, but you're the closest. There's a crash, single vehicle. Uh, the Range Rover you just called in a few minutes ago. Right by the turn-off to your place."

"I'm almost there." I sighed.

"Ambulance and fire are on the way."

I grunted. My day was ruined before it had even started. Or, ended, as the case may be.

The Ponderosa pine at the edge of my property had borne the brunt of the crash. I arrived in time to see the driver exit the vehicle, stumbling out to fall forward into the snow. Long golden-brown waves covered her face as she rose to her hands and knees trying to gain purchase on the slippery surface. I pulled off to the side, turned off the siren but left the lights flashing, and got out.

"Hey, hold still, you could be hurt. I'm coming to help you!" I shouted as I made my way closer.

Clearly panicked, she lurched for the open door of her vehicle and pulled herself up. "Stay away from me!" The door hit my shoulder as she attempted to close it.

"Ma'am, it's okay, you're safe. I'm Detective Caden Barrett, Sweetbriar PD. I'm here to help. An ambulance is on the way."

"Cade?" With a shaking hand, she pushed the thick mass of waves from her face. Gorgeous baby-blue eyes met mine before she burst into tears and fell into my arms. "Oh, thank goodness it's you."

"Charlotte." Shocked was not the right word for how it felt to be holding her again. A jolt of electricity lit me up inside and I gasped, ruffling her hair with my breath. I inhaled deeply, her sweetly familiar floral scent filling my nostrils, and before I could think too hard about it, I pulled her close, tugging her tight against my chest. That same heady rush of sensation shot through my body at the feel of her soft curves finally beneath my hands again. "Are you hurt?" Goosebumps traveled over my flesh as she wrapped her arms around me and pressed herself even closer. Trembling fingers drifted into the hair at the nape of my neck, and I shivered at her touch.

"No. I'm okay, I think. Just shaken up. I wasn't going

that fast when I hit our tree, but the airbag went off." I swallowed hard, trying to steel myself against the rush of memories that currently threatened my good sense. I didn't want to let her go but I had no reason to keep her close.

Soft hands went to my shoulders, pushing me away as she stepped back to lean against the side of the Range Rover. Visible just over her shoulder, the heart I'd carved into the bark when we had first bought this place taunted me. I should have carved an X through it after she left. Or chopped the damn thing down.

"This isn't your car. Where's your Jeep? Why were you driving so fast?" I questioned her. "Was that Subaru following you?" I peppered her with questions about the crash to avoid talking to her about anything real.

Why, after all this time, have you come back to Sweetbriar?

Why did you leave me?

She avoided my eyes as she answered. "No, uh, I mean, I have no idea. Maybe it was road rage? Or they probably thought I was somebody else—"

Blaring sirens filled the air as the fire department's ambulance pulled up next to us, followed by a squad car and a firetruck. Frustrated, I turned to find my younger brother, Levi, stepping out of the driver's side of the ambulance followed by his partner. "Charlotte? Is that you?" His smile was huge as he approached us. "Are you okay? Hey, Cade." I nodded hello to Levi and scowled as Matt, a fellow Sweetbriar PD officer, approached. My moment with Charlotte was obviously over.

Matt called out with a smile, "Yo, Cade, go home and get some sleep. We got it from here."

"Fine. Great. Thanks. Charlotte?" My heart ached as I watched her trembling in the cold. She was as beautiful as ever: freckles on her nose, full pink lips, curves for days, and that same delicate vulnerability that had always hit me straight in the middle of my damn chest every time her eyes had caught mine. Why I wanted to be the one to help her, I did not fully understand, not when she'd so thoroughly smashed my heart beneath her shoe when she walked out of my life over a decade ago.

She looked away. All she said was a meek, "Thank you, Cade."

Levi draped a blanket over her shoulders and led her to the ambulance. She was in good hands with him. I turned my back and headed for my SUV. Of *course* that's all she had to say. I was lucky she'd spoken to me at all, seeing as how we'd been divorced for so long. Not to mention the fact that she had married and divorced someone else during our time apart.

On a giant exhale, I jumped into my car, started it, and drove through the gate adjacent to the Ponderosa pine currently getting way more attention from her busted Range Rover than she'd just given me.

I had known Charlotte was back. You can't live in a town as small as this one and not know all the comings and goings, especially in my line of work. But we'd made an art of avoidance over the last decade; this was only the second time I'd had any contact with her since our divorce. It wasn't easy given both our families were long-time Sweetbriar residents and had known each other for years, but fortunately, everyone was still civil with one another.

Charlotte and I had gone from preschool through graduation together and I had known her brothers almost as well as I knew my own siblings. Her family owned an auto body and mechanic shop right outside of town and I was probably the only person in the area who didn't bring my vehicles to their place. In fact, I hadn't seen any of her family in years except in passing.

After trudging through the snow in my driveway, I made it to my porch. I could see the roof of the coffee shop owned by my older sister, Violet, from here. I should have stopped and grabbed breakfast from her. The thought of cold pizza now turned my stomach, and Netflix? Forget about it. I was too keyed up to relax and I had no one to chill with.

Heaving out a sigh, I unlocked my door and went inside. After kicking off my boots, I headed for the kitchen. My feet slowed over the tile as I approached the island in the center. Palms to my head, I turned in a slow circle. "Damn it," I growled to the empty room, slamming my eyes shut as images of me and Charlotte together burned in the back of my mind. Fucking hell, there was no way I could sleep now, and I had lost my appetite.

I didn't have time for this.

For her or the memories I had worked so hard over the years to banish from my mind.

Or for anything that didn't involve my path toward taking over as chief of police from my father when he retired, which, given the way my mother was pushing him, would be sooner than later.

Why did she have to come back when I'd finally gotten over her? I stalked to my bathroom, tearing my clothes off on the way. A hot shower was what I needed, then I'd go to bed *without* remembering all the nights I'd spent buried inside of her sweet little body, the vows we'd taken, the promises we'd made, the dreams we had shared . . . And I couldn't forget the plans—years' worth of plans—for our future, dead and buried, gone with the stroke of a pen.

The hot spray of water did nothing to calm me down. I turned it to cold, shivering beneath the icy blast as I hurried to wash this entire day away. Trying to scrub thoughts of her out of my mind was useless when I could still feel the soft press of her body against mine.

After slipping into my robe, I cranked up the heater, bypassing my bedroom to fall back on my couch with a plop. I stared at my reflection in the TV screen, my remote sitting beneath it across the room. There were some days when nothing went my way, and apparently this was one of them. On every level. I was well and good into a pity party for one when I punched a throw pillow, then fell to my side. I had just drifted off when pounding on my door woke me up.

"Damn. Seriously?"

"Yo, Cade! Let me in." It was Levi. If he didn't have food or coffee, he would not be invited inside.

Throwing open the door, I greeted him with a grouchy, "What?"

He waved a lavender bag in my face and pushed his way inside. "I brought breakfast from Violet. And a smoothie. You're welcome, sunshine." His knowing smirk was infuriating, but I'd let it go until after I ate. I headed to my room to dress.

His feet were on my coffee table and he was already stuffing his face when I made it back to the living room. Apparently, I had company to entertain.

"Why is your remote way over there, dumbass? Get it before you sit down. Then you can go ahead and ask me."

"Ask you what?" I chucked the remote to him before grabbing the bag full of breakfast he'd brought and taking a huge sip of smoothie. "Thanks, man."

His eyebrows went up as he sipped his coffee and chuckled at my pathetic attempt to keep my feelings to myself. "About Charlotte. She's fine, by the way. I drove her to her dad's place. Her brothers swarmed her like she was near death or something."

"I can imagine." They were probably driving her crazy. She grew up the youngest of six kids and she was the only girl.

"They'll tow her car out to the shop later. You doin' okay? This is the first time you've seen her since she's been home, right?"

"It's fine. I'm fine. I'm over it." I answered, swiping the remote out of his hand and flicking the TV on.

"Sure. Okay." His side eyed skepticism was warranted, but also annoying.

I huffed a beleaguered sigh and avoided his eyes. "I don't want to talk about her," I muttered.

"You never do, and that's fine. I'm only here to help."

"Not to pry?" I arched a brow.

He laughed. "I would never." Levi was a nosy little shit and always had been. He would pry eventually. My entire family was a bunch of meddlers, always up in each other's business. But not me; I stayed out of everyone's way, and I expected the same treatment.

"Mom didn't find out and send you over here?" I prodded. "Ever since she found out about all of it, she's been trying to get me to discuss the fact that Charlotte divorced her husband and asking how I feel about her being single and back in town." I sent him a warning look. "I'm not talking about it, with any of you."

"I'm not here for that, okay?" His eyes softened in sympathy. "The look on your face at the crash site was intense is all. I was worried about you."

My eyebrows lifted in surprise. "Oh, well, thanks. I'm fine. Just tired. I worked all night." I wasn't sure if I wanted to be alone; my memories of Charlotte were coming at me like a freight train, and a distraction could be a good thing. But I was absolutely sure I didn't want to talk about anything that had happened this morning so I turned the volume up on the TV to discourage any more conversation.

Chapter 2
Charlotte

"I swear, you guys. I'm fine. Will one of you drive me home? Please?" Levi finally agreed to drive me somewhere after I had a fit about going to the hospital, but he wouldn't drive me home. He said he didn't want me to be alone, so he brought me to my dad's house instead.

I wanted to be in my own space, in a bathtub full of bubbles, with a huge coffee—where I would most definitely not think about Cade. Then I wanted to get into bed with my laptop to work. What I did *not* want was every single one of my five overprotective older brothers up in my face, grilling me about my little car wreck earlier this morning. And lord help me if they found out I was being followed when it happened. No one in Sweetbriar needed to know about that. I would never hear the end of it, and I was taking care of the problem anyway. It was about to be a moot situation.

"You're not going home. Hunter pulled some of his

chicken soup from the freezer and it's on the stove. You can sleep in your old room tonight." My father was insistent as he tucked a quilt around my shoulders and felt my forehead with the back of his hand.

I pulled my head back. "Dad, I'm fine, I swear. I'm not sick, I hit a tree." I loved my family, but there was only so much hovering I could take before I snapped. I was on a deadline; my next book was due in a month, I had exactly three chapters written, and unfortunately, no matter how hard I wished for it, my books wouldn't write themselves. Stupid science had yet to discover how I could just hook my brain to my laptop and get it done through osmosis or whatever, which meant I had some serious work to do, and I needed to be alone to do it. "I have to write."

"You can write tomorrow. Today you will rest and let your family take care of you. Don't argue with me, you know I'm right."

"I baked cookies last night," Spencer, big brother number five, announced as he set a plate of his secret recipe chocolate chip on the coffee table. "Brody went to Violet's shop to grab you a coffee."

I swiped a cookie and took a bite. "He did?" I reconsidered my desire to go home. Maybe a day with my family would be good for me, especially if there were treats and homemade soup involved. "Will one of you go to my place and snag my laptop?" I supposed I could work here. Cookies made writing easier; every author I knew would agree on that. Plus, if I was being honest with myself, I was still a little shaken up from the crash.

Deacon stood up with a nod.

"Oh, and grab my pajamas from under my pillow. Please?"

His lips quirked up in a grin. "That it?"

"Um . . ." I thought about it. "And grab my pillow too, the one in the pink pillowcase, not the purple one. Thank you, Deacon."

"You got it."

One could argue I had grown up a bit spoiled. My parents had wanted a daughter and after five boys they finally got one—me. But when I was barely a toddler, my mother was diagnosed with stage four breast cancer and within months she had passed away. My dad raised us all on his own. He had a perpetual broken heart and the desire to keep us all close.

Even though I left Sweetbriar to attend college—on a full scholarship, thank you very much—at NYU, then stayed to live in New York City, I always came back to visit. I was here for every holiday and birthday, plus a few weeks every summer. But I stayed close to home whenever I was here. Bumping into Cade or his family in town was never on my to-do list. That was a scenario that had awkward written all over it. The only exception was his mother. We spoke from time to time over the years. She used to be like a mother to me, as well as my writing mentor, and I was thankful that I was able to keep her in my life, albeit sporadically. We had an unspoken agreement to never, ever talk about Cade. Somehow it worked.

Plus, *ouch*—part of him remained with me, like a pokey little thorn. No matter how hard I had tried to forget about him, he was always there. I was afraid he'd always be lurking somewhere in the cockles of my heart, the comparison for any man I would ever date.

He was my first love; we'd known each other since pre-school, but the eighth grade Sadie Hawkins Day dance was when everything had changed. I took my shot and he'd said yes. We were together all through high school and got married right after graduation. We'd divorced a few years later.

But after the divorce, despite what I had intended when I left, I had never been brave enough to take another shot. Years went by, we both moved on, and then it was too late. I couldn't bear the thought of moving back to Sweetbriar and not being with him, so I stayed in New York and hid out at my dad's place whenever I visited my family.

"Who's running the shop?" My father owned a mechanic-slash-auto body shop right outside of Sweetbriar, called Cassidy's Automotive. All my brothers—Hunter, Deacon, Tucker, Brody, and Spencer—worked for him. They rebuilt, restored, and repaired cars, trucks, and motorcycles—anything with a motor and the ability to go *vroom*. They were similar in looks, like my parents had cut and pasted them into existence: all tall, with dark brown hair, light blue eyes just like mine, and muscular from working hard with my dad at the shop.

I, on the other hand, had never given the first crap about any of that stuff. I'd always wanted to be a writer, so I did it. I had ten *New York Times* best sellers and was working on my eleventh. I wrote murder mysteries featuring my heroine, Detective Adaline Paige.

Did I sometimes creep myself out? Yep.

Did I sleep with the lights on and a baseball bat by my bed? Also yep.

What can I say? I was so good at what I did, I terrified myself on a daily basis. My imagination was ridiculous. I was also addicted to true crime podcasts, Stephen King novels, and had done several ride alongs with my various NYPD research buddies. People are hella messed up and that is a fact. I had endless disturbing ideas for books filed away in my twisty brain.

"Hunter is there. Do you want to talk about what happened? After Levi dropped you off, he told me Cade was the first responder. I bet it brought up memories for you."

"Yeah, I hadn't expected to see him. I wasn't prepared."

"Oh, honey. Come here." He held his arms out, I scooted over and leaned into him. My dad gave the best hugs, I always imagined being held by a big teddy bear would feel similar. He was six-foot-five with a broad chest and huge arms. His wavy salt and pepper hair was tied back in a ponytail, and for as long as I could remember, he'd had a full beard and mustache. He looked like a murderous biker but acted like a nineteen-fifties era housewife. Once, when I was four, he shaved his beard off and I hadn't recognized him. I cried until he dug up his and my mother's wedding photos to prove who he was. He'd grown it back and had kept it ever since. "How was it?" he asked.

I couldn't describe how I had felt this morning with Cade. not when I was still trying to process it for myself. "I don't know what to say. I thought I'd be able to handle seeing him again after I finally bit the bullet and went to Violet's shop for coffee over Christmas to get the lay of the land. But I was wrong. It was . . ." *Intense, nostalgic, heartbreaking.* I bit my lip and looked away.

"It's good to talk about these things, Charlotte," he encouraged. "After everything you two went through in the past, a run-in had to be hard, especially since a lack of love was never the problem for you. Feelings are coming back up, right?"

"I don't know what to feel yet." That was a lie. I'd felt a lot of things when I was back in Cade's arms, none of which I wanted to talk about with my dad.

And shamefully, I wanted to feel it all again. No man had ever made me respond like Cade could. One look from him set my body on fire, sent my heart into over-drive, and turned my brain into love-drunk mush.

As for being in his arms again? I hadn't wanted to leave. I'd had to force myself away from him. He made me feel safe when I had been beyond scared. Plus, he looked as handsome as he always had.

I'd never thought I was one of those women who was attracted to a man in uniform, but I was wrong. He was sexy as hell in his Sweetbriar PD jacket, dark jeans, and that thick belt with his badge and gun clipped to it. Plus, his body was ridiculous now; it felt like I had pressed myself against a brick wall when we hugged.

Maybe I should wreck another car and see if he would show up? I mean, I was surrounded by cars in various states of repair right now. I had plenty to choose from.

He sighed. "I get it. You probably don't want to talk to your old man about stuff like this. But make sure not to keep it all inside, okay?"

"I won't."

He hesitated. "And honey?"

"Yeah, Dad?"

"I miss you around here, all of us do, and I can't help but wish you'd stay for good this time."

I let my eyes drift around the familiar living room and over the dark wood floors, big comfy furniture, and the family pictures. So many pictures . . . "I missed you guys too. And—"

His eyes lit up on the "and," and he nodded, encouraging me to finish.

"I'll think about it this time, I promise."

"It would mean the world to me, to all of us." He got up and flicked the TV on for me. "I don't want you getting off that couch today, princess. I'll be at the shop. I have a few engine rebuilds on the schedule and can't get behind, otherwise I'd be here to take care of you myself. Text me if you need anything, and at least one of your brothers will be here in the house all day. Put 'em to work." He winked.

"Okay, Dad." The shop was on the same property as the house. My brothers, except for Hunter and Deacon, the two oldest, still lived here with my dad. I would be safe here with them around.

For now, anyway.

This morning shook me up. And I doubted I'd get unshaken anytime soon.

Because I had a stalker.

I also had a couple of police reports and a seemingly useless restraining order against one Mr. Douglas Winthrop, pain in my ass and current ruiner of my life.

Trent, my college best friend and second ex-husband, suggested I get out of New York for a while to let Winthrop cool down and hopefully forget about me.

He had also encouraged me to take Krav Maga classes and buy a taser, both of which I did. My taser is cute and purple and I carry it in my purse. I also have a mini keychain pepper spray canister and am not afraid to spray the shit out of old Douggie McStalker if he gets in my face again. My new toys, my brand-new set of self-defense and fighting skills, and the fact that I grew up with five older brothers meant I could kick some ass, if need be.

Trent and I had always been platonic, even during our marriage. He'd needed a wife to claim an inheritance from his old-fashioned, stick-up-his-butt grandfather. We stayed married for a year, Trent got his fifty million dollars, then bada-bing-bada-boom—divorce. It was straight out of a rom com, except neither one of us had gotten laid and we never fell in love. Mostly, we just lived together in his fancy penthouse apartment and ate take-out in front of the television every night—much like we did before we got married.

Ironically, Trent had sort of become my stalker's stalker after I left New York. He kept an eye on him for me and made sure he stayed in New York so I could have some breathing room back here in Sweetbriar. Hiding out in my hometown, finishing my book, and hanging out with my family would be just the thing to get him to forget about me. Then I could go back to New York and continue living my life.

So far, so good. My nom de plume—Keli, my middle name, and Marlowe, my mom's maiden name—still concealed my identity, and he hadn't yet managed to track me to Sweetbriar.

But the crash this morning had me worried. Trent would have been on a plane the second he had any new information. At the very least, he would have called to let me know to watch out. I had called and texted and hadn't heard from him yet, which was freaking me out.

I had rented a townhouse when I came back but in this moment I couldn't help thinking maybe I should have chosen a bigger place instead. One with a high fence and a yard that I could put a few guard dogs in, and perhaps a piranha-filled moat with a big-ass portcullis. My paranoid imagination sometimes got the best of me. It served me well as a writer, but it sucked when I was trying to fall asleep in the dark of night.

I curled up on my side as I blindly watched whatever was on TV. The fear I tried to keep on the outer edges of my thoughts had encroached into my daily life again this morning and it pissed me off.

I had lost my focus, which meant I wouldn't be able to write today. I couldn't even relax in my childhood home for a minute while surrounded by my five brothers and father who all still treated me like a baby and would stomp anyone who messed with me into the ground.

Apparently, it was foolish to think I could ditch him by moving back home. I'd had a few blessed months without Douglas Winthrop's weirdo stalker schtick, and it had been wonderful. *Ugh*, even his name was creepy. On principle, I didn't like to say it or think it. I didn't want to give it the power to influence my life.

I didn't know for sure he was the one in the Subaru behind me this morning, but I would be an idiot if I didn't assume it was. And I was nobody's fool.

He was just a normal reader at first. Then he'd upped his game to rabid super fan, leaving obsessive comments on my social media, followed by letters sent to my publisher, then finally following me home after a book signing to stand on the sidewalk outside my house later that night with handwritten signs, á la the *Love, Actually* cards-in-the-doorway scene. But, too bad for his wacko ass, he lacked the charm of Andrew Lincoln, and instead of opening the door I'd called the cops. He hadn't tried to hurt me physically or break into my house (yet?) but he scared me all the same and I was sick of it.

It wasn't even me he was fixated on; it was the character I'd created for my books. I wrote a series of big city murder mysteries called *The Adaline Paige Files*. He was obsessed with Detective Adaline Paige, my heroine—not me. Apparently, he thought she was real. His letters were addressed to her, and when he showed up on my porch, he had called me by her name. Clearly, he was a delusional wackadoodle.

Time was passing too fast. I wanted to hear from Trent; he had to be okay. I wanted the peace I had rediscovered to continue. I didn't want to tell Cade or Matt or any of the other police officers in town about my stalker. And I really didn't want to tell my family. I probably should have been honest this morning, but the tiny chance that it could have been some random driver with a horrible case of road rage held me back. I was enjoying my freedom here and I didn't want it to end.

Shaking off the fear for the moment—because screw being scared—I got up and headed to the fridge for a glass of milk to go along with the cookies.

"I have a bone to pick with you." I spun as Brody, big brother number four, entered the kitchen. He sat at the table and slid my take-out coffee toward the empty seat across from him.

Nervous laughter escaped before I could stop it. "I didn't do it, I swear," I joked as I joined him at the table.

He didn't laugh. "I ran into my buddy, Matt, at Violet's while I was getting your coffee. Did you leave out something about your accident when you were on the phone with Dad this morning?" An eyebrow ticked up as he waited for my answer.

"Uhhh . . ." Yes, I did, and I clearly should have known better. This entire damn town had a big mouth. It was like a great gaping maw of information, constantly spewing people's personal facts at anyone who would listen. It was impossible to have any privacy in a small town like Sweetbriar.

"Someone was following you, Charlotte. Didn't you think we should know about that?"

"Probably." I avoided his eyes and slunk down in my chair. "I mean, I guess so."

"You guess so," he scoffed. "Well, luckily, they caught her. Matt arrested her about an hour ago."

"*Her?*" I exhaled ten different sighs of relief all rolled into one big ass puff of air as I deflated further in my chair and took a huge swig of my iced mocha. "They caught *her?*" A massive smile split my face as I slapped a palm on the table. "Who was it? Tell me." Maybe I was okay. Maybe he hadn't tracked me down here in Sweetbriar and I could be normal for a little while longer. Either that, or I had acquired another stalker. I wrinkled my nose at that unpleasant thought.

He shook his head, grinning at my odd reaction but didn't question me about it since I was, indeed, an odd duck, and by now he was used to it. "It was a woman named Bethany Rhodes and I'm not even getting into the gossip surrounding her—you can ask around town if you want to know. She thought your Range Rover was Violet's."

"As in Cade's big sister? Coffee shop Violet? Who would ever want to hurt her? She's awesome." I held my drink aloft as evidence. "This coffee is a freakin' masterpiece of caffeination. Jeez."

He shot me a look. "Her husband's ex-mistress-slash-ex-fiancé, for one."

"Ohhhh, snap." I guess when you avoided people, you also avoided the gossip about them. I had no idea Violet had been through something like that.

"Yeah. Well, she says she didn't want to hurt anyone . . ." He rolled his eyes and sipped his coffee.

I was indignant. "She tailgated me right into a freakin' tree. She forced me get up close and personal with my ex-husband before I was emotionally ready." I stood and waved an angry finger in the air. "I'll sue her ass off. Plus, that car was new, Brody. And let's not even get into the fact that she scared the ever-loving shit out of me. And, god, I hope the tree is okay. I have always loved that big ol' tree."

He chuckled. "Hunter is on his way to tow your Range Rover back to the shop. You can ask him how the tree is doing when he gets here."

"*Ugh.*" I slunk back into my chair. "Junk the car or donate it to someone who needs a free car. I never want to see it again."

"Do you want a loaner? Or you could take your old Jeep. It's in the garage. I brought the keys just in case."

"Thank you, Brody. This is fantastic. I'm going home." I grabbed my coffee and stood, holding my hand out and wriggling my fingers for the keys. "Tell Dad bye for me."

He huffed a laugh. "No way. You tell him. Better yet, go park your butt back on the couch. Let's not get the argument started."

"Fine, but only because I don't want to fight. And Deacon is bringing my stuff anyway. Plus, that soup smells delicious and Dad told me to put you all to work. Now what else can I make you do for me?" I teased.

His eyes softened. "Baby sister, you know we'd all do anything for you. I'm glad you're okay. And I'm even more glad you're here for a while. Who knows? Maybe we can convince you to stay this time. And what about Trent? Is he coming out for a visit too? I miss that dude."

"Maybe sometime next month. If he can take time off from work."

"Awesome. Speaking of work, I have to get a move on and go help Dad." He ruffled my hair and kissed the top of my head as he passed, heading to the back door. "Love you. Now get back to that couch."

Gosh, I had the best brothers ever. "I love you too, Brody, and I'm glad I'm here. I missed you guys."

My pocket vibrated and I quickly snatched my cell.

Trent: I'm okay. What's happening? Are you okay? Bonehead Douglas is having lunch at Mickey D's right now. You're still good.

. . .

Charlotte: Nothing. Just a fender bender. I'm awesome now. I got worried over nothing. Talk more later.

With a smile, I went back to zoning out in front of the TV. Looks like I'd be enjoying more down time in good old Sweetbriar.

Chapter 3
Cade

It had been a week since the crash. I was slowly losing my mind to the pull of the past and I was frustrated with myself for not being able to control my emotions. Now that I had finally seen Charlotte, I found myself wanting to see her again, and it pissed me off that she was never anywhere around town. I couldn't seem to run into her despite trying shamefully hard to do so. My house wasn't even safe from the reawakened memories since we'd lived here together after we got married. I tossed to my other side, shoving an arm beneath my head as I reached for my cell phone to check the time.

It was way too early to be awake. The crash and our conversation after it still played on a loop in my mind. I couldn't let it go. Charlotte had been terrified; I'd seen it in her eyes. She'd denied to my face being followed, but Matt's report said otherwise. She would have no reason to lie to me unless she had something to hide, like she thought she knew who was following her and didn't want anyone to know. And if someone had been chasing her, was she in danger? Or could it be something less serious?

Vowing to get to the bottom of whatever trouble Charlotte was in, I threw off my covers and sat on the edge of the bed. It was barely dawn and I was exhausted. She was all I could think about and sleeping had become impossible.

I was off work, but like every other day this past week, I didn't want to be stuck in the house where I would undoubtedly torture myself all day with memories of her. I got dressed to head to Violet's where I could eat breakfast and formulate a plan. I needed something to do all day, because just like when Charlotte had first left me, I couldn't stand to be alone with my thoughts.

The early morning sun melted the ice on the roads so the trip into town was quick. My stomach growled, my need for food and caffeine almost as intense as my desire to get her out of my fucking head—for good this time.

Violet's shop was located in a strip mall in the center of town. Like most of the other buildings in Sweetbriar it was designed with a mountain aesthetic in mind; think dark wood and natural stone facades with pine trees and evergreen shrubs planted in every spare patch of dirt. I swung into a spot in front of the shop and got out, the crisp breeze making me shiver, and hurried inside to get warm. It was early, so the line was long. Everyone in Sweetbriar got their coffee here. Violet was good enough that eventually she ran all other coffee shops out of town.

"Earth to Cade." Violet waved a hand in front of my face.

"What?" I mumbled as I looked around. In a daze, I'd made it to the front of the line without noticing.

She chuckled. "What's eating you? Charlotte, right? Go to the corner table with Mom and I'll be right over. You want the usual, right?"

"Uh, yeah. Thanks, Vi." I headed for the table Violet kept reserved for my mother. She wrote romance novels for a living and most of her newest works were done right here in the shop. She always said people watching inspired her. I wondered if Charlotte felt the same way about her own writing. I kind of hoped not. Charlotte wrote murder mysteries; what could possibly inspire her by watching people?

Mom was hugely successful. In fact, she had mentored Charlotte when we were in high school, helping her hone her writing skills and later helping her find an agent, stuff like that.

"Cade, sit." She moved her laptop bag from the chair next to her and patted it. "How are you doing, honey? I know you're off today. I was going to bring you dinner tonight so we can chat. I heard everything from Levi."

"Of course you did." I forced a laugh. "I'm fine. I'm over it."

"We both know that isn't true." Her eyes, shining behind her black cat eye lenses, were soft on mine as she patted my hand. "But I'm not here to be nosy. I'm here to make sure you're okay."

"Thanks, Mom. I'm fine." I looked up as Violet placed a blueberry muffin and a coffee in front of me.

Violet looked at me skeptically. "Okay. Sure. You're just fine and dandy."

Frustrated, I dragged a hand through my hair. "Why don't any of you believe me? I *am* fine, really." Over the last week, each one of my siblings—and I had seven of them—let it be known they thought I was full of shit, accusing me of lying about my feelings for Charlotte. I'd gotten quite an earful, and it was split fifty-fifty as to whether I was lying to them or to myself.

"Don't blame us for being observant," Violet snarked before taking a seat next to me. "Denial isn't good for anyone, Cade. Let us help you." She stabbed a straw into her iced coffee, an eyebrow shooting up as she studied my face and took a sip.

"I'm not in denial." That was not a lie, and the fact that I didn't want them to know how I really felt about Charlotte being back in town proved it.

"Don't argue with your brother, Violet. If he wants to say he's fine, then he's fine until he needs us." Her eyes got huge as she peered over my shoulder. "Don't look," she hissed.

Instinctively, I turned to look. Charlotte stood in the doorway; her eyes shot to mine while a hesitant smile crossed her face. She was dressed for a run—black leggings, long sleeved thermal T-shirt, and a puffy purple vest. She was gorgeous with her hair in a high ponytail and her cheeks flushed bright pink from exertion. I lifted a hand in greeting before turning back to face my mother.

"You never were a good listener," she muttered while Violet laughed.

"I've got to get back to work. You'll be okay." Vi patted my shoulder before making her way back to the counter.

"Right, she's gone. Now, we can talk."

"There's nothing to talk about," I insisted, unwrapping my muffin and taking a bite. "She's been back for a couple months. No one wanted to talk about her with me when she first got to town. What is up with the interrogation now?"

Her head tilted and her eyebrows furrowed while she studied my face. "You hadn't seen her yet. You went back inside your lonely, divorced Caden bubble and hid out at home. You haven't been on a date since she came back. Don't think we haven't noticed. This is bothering you more than you let on."

I shrugged and sipped my coffee while having an internal debate as to whether or not I wanted to get into a discussion about my love life with my mother. I decided on *not*.

"Look, honey. This is one situation I'm not going to meddle in." My eyes went wide as my head jerked back on my neck. My mother was a notorious matchmaker; so was my sister Violet, for that matter. I'd have to keep my eye on them both. "Cade, I have to be honest with you. I've kept in touch with Charlotte over the years. We didn't speak often, but I never told you because—"

Holding up a hand, I stopped her. "She loved you and she needed you. I'm not angry about it. Why should you remove her from your life because my marriage with her didn't work out?" Her sigh of relief broke my heart. I took her hand across the table. It bothered me a little, but not enough to get angry over.

"Darling, I'm so relieved you feel this way. Thank you. I was worried you'd be hurt, and I would never want to hurt you. It's just—I have always thought of her like another daughter and I didn't want to abandon her entirely."

"I'm not hurt. You two were always close." I gestured to her laptop. "Is she going to join you here? To write or whatever?"

"We hadn't talked about it. I mean, this is Violet's place and she's your sister—"

"I really don't want to be like that anymore—my side of town and hers. Especially since she's planting roots here again. I should make it a point to stop avoiding her. This is different than when she was visiting for a holiday or on vacation. She has a townhouse this time. I can be an adult about it as much as she's trying to be—that's why she's been coming in here lately, isn't it? To get to know you all again. Plus, if she's going to stay in town, where else would she get her coffee?"

"Yes, all of that is definitely part of it. There's probably some curiosity as well."

"Curiosity? About what?"

"You, of course, silly."

"It's been over a decade, Mom," I scoffed. "I doubt that. Plus, she left me, remember?"

Her eyes narrowed. "It wasn't as simple as her merely *leaving*, and you know that, Caden."

Again, I shrugged off her opinion. To me it *was* that simple. I'd loved her with my whole heart and it hadn't been enough to make her stay. "Let's not get into it," I suggested.

"But, Cade, I—"

Out of the corner of my eye I saw Charlotte head to the door with her order.

"Good luck with the writing today. Love you, Mom." I gathered my trash and stood. "I have somewhere to be." While I didn't quite storm out, my exit had an unintended dramatic flair that embarrassed me.

Halfway to her car, I stopped her with a hand on her arm, flinching at the burst of electricity that shot through me at the contact. I swiftly pulled away. "Hey, Charlotte? Can we talk?"

Surprised eyes met mine as she turned. "Sure."

I needed to get to the bottom of her lie about being followed before the crash. She knew the mountain roads, how to drive in the snow and be safe. If someone was in my town threatening the people who lived here, it was my duty to put a stop to it.

Especially if the one being threatened was Charlotte.

Frustrated, I shook off my last thought. Bottom line, it didn't matter who was in danger, it was my job to keep everyone safe.

The problem was where to start. Asking her direct questions would only serve to make her suspicious. She had lied to me before, I was sure of it, and she was not the type of person to lie for no reason, or even at all. Whatever had compelled her to downplay what happened had to be serious.

The wind kicked up, blowing a loose curl over her eye. My mouth opened, but nothing came out. I wanted to brush that curl back in the worst way. Instead, I ran a hand through my own hair and looked away with a short sigh.

"For someone who just asked to speak to me, you're not very talkative." I didn't have to look at her to see the expression she wore. I'd seen it many times before: a small grin tipped higher on one side, her head tilted, blue eyes sparkling with mirth as she teased me.

A glance down at her confirmed I was correct. I tensed as nostalgia smacked me in the back of the head. "I'm sorry. I—it's good you came home, Charlotte. Everyone missed you. About the car accident—"

"Thanks. Uh, you know I'm renting a townhouse over on Pine Street?" She was fidgety, trying to deflect my question like she had anticipated what I would ask. Or maybe the caffeine had just hit her system and she was jittery because of that. It would take me a few more minutes to read her right, given I was about ten years or so out of practice.

"I know. My entire family told me. Guess you're sticking around then?" I winked, knowing it used to get her flustered. I wanted her off balance so she would answer my questions.

Her cheeks turned pink. "That figures. And yeah, I'll be around. I thought I should warn you." She let out a surprised laugh. "Dang, there really are no secrets in this town."

"News travels fast around here. Speaking of that—"

"I heard you're a detective now, and maybe in line to take over for your dad, too?" The wind blew her wavy ponytail over her shoulder. I forced my eyes away.

I had always loved her soft hair, how it felt against my bare skin, running my hands into it as I kissed her—*damn it,* now I was the one who was off balance. Clearing my throat, I forced that line of thought out of my head and reminded myself I had a job to do.

"That's the plan. So, Matt mentioned that you knew you were being followed, is that right?"

"Violet invited me to her monthly book club, to uh, talk about my books, maybe sign a few. Are you okay with that? I haven't said yes. I wanted to check with you first."

Cutting off a frustrated sigh I answered. "Yeah, that's fine. You don't have to check with me about anything. You're entitled to be here living your life just as much as I am. Are you going to answer me?"

Her eyes shifted to the side, and she took a huge sip of her coffee. "Um, about what?"

"We need to talk about the accident."

"No, we don't. It was someone named Bethany Rhodes behind me. You know all about it, don't you? And I'm sure you know what's in the police report, right? I told Matt everything I saw."

"Are you sure? Sometimes when people get shaken up, things get forgotten." I searched her eyes for something—for what, exactly, I'm not sure. "It's normal, Charlotte. I want to help. If anything is amiss or you're in trouble somehow, I'm here for you. Did you suspect someone else was following you?"

"Cade, nobody else was there. Okay?"

"Okay, Charlotte." I studied her face, still convinced she wasn't telling me everything, but willing to drop the subject until I could find another approach. "I'm glad you're back. I'll see you around town." Getting away from her was imperative. Leftover feelings wrapped inside of a new worry for her safety flooded my mind and clouded my judgement. I needed to be alone to sort through them, to make sure my feelings for her weren't leading me astray.

"Bye, Cade." Her voice trailed after me as I booked it to my car. I couldn't get away fast enough.

Chapter 4
Charlotte

*W*hat was that? My hand went to my neck, gathering the chain I always wore and running it through my fingers as he hurried to his police SUV. In a daze I watched him get inside, start it, and drive away. This moment felt almost as bad as when I had watched him leave the attorney's office after we signed the divorce papers. My stomach lurched and I tossed the rest of my iced coffee and blueberry muffin in the trash can on the corner. My appetite was gone.

I hadn't lied, but I hadn't told him the entire truth either. Lies of omission were often just as bad. Guilt ate at me as I got into my car. I was tempted to drive back to the Sweetbriar High School track to run off these rotten feelings. But running out my emotions hadn't worked this morning, so why would it work now? Damn it, I should have stayed away, found another place to hide out.

Coming back to Sweetbriar was a mistake.

He was smooth. The years had polished him to a shine. Cool, collected, and handsome as all hell, he had asked me questions as I shivered from what I was still trying to convince myself was the cold. But deep down I knew it was him. He affected me just as much as he always had, and it stung that he didn't feel the same curiosity about me. After the accident, falling into his arms and wanting to stay there was not a fluke born of fear. It was obviously a resurgence of all the feelings I had tried so hard to bury, and now I knew for sure at least a few of them were back.

There was no time for this. I had a book due and a freaking stalker to deal with. There was already too much on my plate; adding leftover Cade feels to it would be ridiculous and dumb and a waste of time because he obviously didn't care about me anymore.

I mean, he hadn't cared enough when I left Sweetbriar for NYU to wait for me. I'd asked him for time, and he'd asked me for a divorce.

Brushing away the burgeoning hurt, I turned onto Main Street and aimlessly drove through town, filling myself up with bittersweet memories over each street I turned onto.

Eff this.

Wasting my feelings on a man who didn't care about me beyond what I could provide for his police report was foolish. Motor moping around town was a waste of precious work time—and gas.

I pulled into the Quickbriar Stop and Go for a fill up and some breakfast. My appetite had returned and I was getting perilously close to unleashing my hangry alternate personality all over the unsuspecting citizens of Sweetbriar.

Plus, I had so much freaking work to do. Sleep was about to become a fond memory. My caffeine intake was about to triple, and I needed to stock up on writing snacks.

On a mission, I parked at the pump, told the attendant to fill 'er up, and marched through the glass double doors. I snagged a little basket and headed for cooler cases in the back—*come to mama, Diet Dr. Pepper*. I had a freakin' book to finish. Detective Adaline Paige and her deadline of doom waited for no one.

"Hey, Charlotte!" Startled, I turned back to the front counter, snagging a Snickers and a bag of M&M's from the rack on the way.

"Hey, Elizabeth! What's up? How's your sister?" Elizabeth's family owned this place. Her sister, Gwen, was my Sweetbriar bestie, from pre-school to present day. We were supposed to have lunch and reconnect, but life stuff—otherwise known as her four kids—kept coming up to get in the way and I hadn't seen her yet.

She gestured to a customer angrily stomping to the self-serve soda fountain. "I was trying to convince Mrs. Pain-In-My-Ass that I do not have Marlboros in the back," she quietly hissed as she air-quoted 'the back.' "I don't know what the hell people think we keep back there—Narnia? An elven workshop?" Her eyes rolled in comic annoyance. "My fricking purse is back there hanging on a hook next to the employee schedule on a jacked-up clipboard and a few expired Snapples, jeez. Anyway, Gwen is good, kids are good, the ex-husband is a dick-face loser as per usual. But you'd better text her back soon if you don't want her all up in your face demanding details about the accident, know what I mean? Word about that has traveled all the way around town. You know how it is around here."

"Gotcha. I'll text her later. I don't suppose you have Tapatío Doritos back there? No one ever stocks those." I smirked as I gestured to the back room. "I need spicy writing fuel for Adaline's extra spicy scenes."

"Dude. I always have those, they're my fave. Your spicy scenes are my fave too." She laughed. "If you don't find them on the shelf, check the box by the display. And next time you come in, I'm going to have my copy of *Beg for It* for you to sign."

"You got it! I'm doing Vi's book club soon. I hope you'll come."

"You know I wouldn't miss that!"

"Awesome." I meandered through the store, stuffing my basket with various Hostess, Little Debbie, and Lay's products on my way to the Doritos in the rear corner. It was a sad fact that junk food made me write better. Or maybe the added sugar and preservatives did stuff to my brain chemistry and bumped up my creativity. I wasn't going to question it. If it ain't broke, don't fix it. That was my motto.

The bell over the door *dinged* as someone entered the store. "Hey, Elizabeth." My ears pricked.

It was Cade.

I couldn't handle another run-in today. My heart was already hurting from the one earlier. The more I saw him, the harder it was to shove him out of my brain, and that's what I had to do in order to regain at least part of my focus since Monsieur Assface Von Stalker was hogging up a good portion of the rest, dang it.

"Shoot," I muttered as I rushed to the cardboard pyramid of Dorito bags and tried to squeeze my booty behind it. My purse slipped from my shoulder, jostling the basket from my elbow straight into the display, knocking it to the ground. "Dang it, damn it, crap."

Now what?

I contemplated burying myself in the pile of chips but rejected the thought as I looked up; the security mirror showed Elizabeth trying not to laugh as she watched my antics.

Just fricking great.

Cade's eyes were bright as he fought a smile and headed my way. "I'll help her pick it up, Elizabeth. Those Doritos are a hazard, aren't they?"

"Don't I know it, dude. Thanks," she called out. "Uh, did you find the Tapatío flavor, Charlotte?"

Frantically, I looked around, snagging a bag off the floor. "Yes! It was precariously perched, and I am clumsy. I'm so sorry." Her attempt to cover my bumbling effort to hide from Cade was admirable. I made a mental note to bring her some swag when I came back to sign her book. Us girls had to stick together.

"Charlotte," he greeted as he approached.

"Coming to my rescue again, Cade. You're such a

hero," I deadpanned. Lately, being in this town was like taking a body blow with each step I took. Pretty soon I'd be riddled with bruises.

His smile slipped. "I do what I can." Bending, he righted the cardboard display and avoided my eyes.

Immediately, I felt bad. "I didn't mean anything by—"

"Of course you didn't. Don't worry about it."

"Okay . . ."

Silently, we made quick work of cleaning up the Doritos while I tried to think of something to say to him or a way to escape this situation without making a bigger ass of myself than I already had.

I spared him a furtive glance from the corner of my eye.

He was unaffected.

Stone-faced.

Probably angry with me too. He knew I hadn't told the truth about the accident, and he was a cop. I had lied to a cop, just like a criminal would. I was his bad guy du jour—that's all this was.

We were just two people who used to mean everything to each other, no big deal. Our history filled up this entire stupid town, but those days were long over. He'd moved on and so had I, I guess.

No. I did.

I had moved on.

I moved to New York and built a life there.

And clearly, he would never forgive me for it. Or forget how much I had hurt him when I left.

The deep timbre of his voice interrupted my self-pitying reverie, sending a bolt of startled electricity to my heart. "Maybe we should have lunch? Catch up a little bit?"

My jaw dropped and my eyes shot to his. "The fuck?"

He burst out laughing. "Lunch? You know, the meal you eat between breakfast and dinner?"

"Huh?" My nose wrinkled as I studied his face, searching for the ulterior motive that had to be lurking somewhere beneath the surface of his benign smile.

He gestured to my junk food filled basket on the floor. "Or do you already have lunch plans today?"

"What?" I followed his pointy finger to my basket. "No, those are just writing snacks, for later. Um, you want to have lunch?"

His broad shoulders went up in a shrug along with one eyebrow as he regarded my stunned expression. "I try to eat it every day."

"With me?"

"Yeah, with you." He rolled his eyes with a chuckle. "We're both here in town, right?" I shrugged in answer, still too confused to reply with words. "We should find a way to get along, don't you think? In case you forgot, Sweetbriar is a small town, Charlotte."

"Well, being awkward around each other serves no purpose." I threw a hand out, gesturing to the mess I'd made. "Just look what I did to the Doritos, for eff's sake." I knew he wanted to grill me some more and I should say no to lunch. But I was fascinated by the various and sexy ways in which he had changed while I was gone so I hesitated, biting my lip. "Um, okay. We can have lunch together."

His honey brown eyes crinkled at the corner as he grinned. "Great. Should we meet at Holloway's?"

I frowned. He knew I never went there when I was in town. His aunt and cousins owned that place and we had avoided each other's turf ever since the divorce. But he also knew I used to be addicted to their hamburgers, and their tater tots. They made pretty great banana milkshakes too. And their selection of beer was top notch.

And how could I forget the pièce de résistance? We had our first date at Holloway's, and so many memories—an entire plethora of Cade and Charlotte memories—lived in their back corner booth. Our past Holloway dates together ran the gamut between innocent thirteen-year-olds sharing a milkshake to dinner for newlywed eighteen-year-olds who may or may not have enjoyed a finger-bang beneath the table.

My eyelids narrowed as I tilted up my chin and looked at him from the corner of my eye. This was definitely suspicious behavior, but I was too intrigued to fight my curious instincts and give him the third degree. "Yeah, I guess I can meet you there, probably. What time were you thinking of?" My agreement was hesitant, and he was trying not to laugh, I could tell.

He grinned that sexy, small half-grin that in the past would have led to a make out session or a quick bang up against the wall. But today? Not so much. I cleared my throat and looked away.

He was already stimulating my top five erogenous zones by just standing there doing nothing. I did not need to see that sexy *"You're so cute, Charlotte"* smirk smile he always did whenever he found my dorkiness entertaining.

And my heart, *gah!* That little betrayer had started getting all hectic in my chest every time he got near me.

"Noon?" he suggested with an amused shake of his head.

High noon.

Like a shoot-out or a duel.

I would have to be sure to mentally prepare for his questions.

He planned to ply me with burgers and beer and all the rest of my favorites. If he ordered cheese tots, I would have to kick him in the shin on principle. He wanted to loosen me up and get me to spill my guts, but I was on to him and his sneaky law enforcement ways. Heck, I wrote murder mysteries and that had to count for something, right? At least I hoped so.

Curiosity and his burning hot sex-appeal battled with my good sense as I contemplated lunch with him. Unfortunately, I was weak and horny, not to mention hungry and battling a serious craving for a good burger ever since the mention of Holloway's a few minutes ago, so I made an inevitable bad choice and agreed to meet him. "I'll see you at noon, Cade."

He flicked two fingers out in a wave and headed for the door. "Until then." He winked and strode for the exit.

"Whatever," I mumbled under my breath. He really

needed to quit winking at me. He'd done it twice today and I could take no more. Winking made me want to do bad, bad things to him, something he was likely well aware of based on the historical fact that every time one of his eyelids dropped down both of my legs usually dropped open.

Quickly, I grabbed the rest of my necessities and made my way to the front of the store to pay for my snacks. I plunked my basket on the counter with a grimace.

Elizabeth started to ring me up. "You're in trouble, girl."

I added a few bags of Skittles and a pack of Hubba Bubba to my haul. "You got that right, dude."

But did I save future Charlotte from pain and confusion and text him to cancel?

Hell to the nope.

Present Charlotte was a bonehead and way too curious to back out.

Chapter 5
Cade

L*unch time.* I stood to the side of the dark wooden door of Holloway's waiting to get my heart run through a blender again.

What the hell was I doing?

This was the stupidest idea I'd had in ages. She was never going to answer my questions about the crash, and I was never going to be able to keep resisting the urge to—to, what? Ask her out for a real date? We'd been *out*. Hell, we'd been married. I'd been in and out and all over her for fuck's sake. And hell, I wanted to do it all again.

I blew out a sigh, dragging a hand over my beard as I contemplated sending her a text to cancel. Was her phone number even the same?

Damn, this was going to hurt in so many different ways. Emotionally, as well as physically, since my dick wanted to get reacquainted with Charlotte almost as much as my heart and my brain did. There was no way it could ever happen. Been there, done that, had the divorce papers to prove it.

We wanted different things out of life and that was an irrevocable fact. She was all city girl, big career, with bigger plans for even more, and I was one-hundred-percent mountain cop who loved my small town and never wanted to leave. Who was I to try to keep her here? She was meant for so much more than me and the simple life I could give her.

Too late.

She pulled up in her old Jeep and I tried to keep my jaw from dropping as she got out. Her hair was down, longer now than when we'd been together, but she still had that one curly lock that insisted on falling over her eyes. I shoved my hands into my pockets as the familiar urge to push it out of her face tempted me. She had changed into a soft pink sweater, high heeled boots, and a pair of tight jeans.

Please don't turn around.

No such luck. With a twist and a half turn, the delectable curve of her ass caught my eye as she grabbed a jacket out of the Jeep, slipped it on, then headed my way, waving and smiling as she walked. God, I wouldn't mind taking a bite out of her ass for lunch instead of a burger.

Stupidly, I had thought breaking the ice over a meal together would make things less awkward between us, make it easier to be in the same town again, and maybe make it easier on my mother as well. I knew Mom had always adored Charlotte as a kindred writing spirit back when we were together and I didn't want to stand in the way of their friendship. Now that Charlotte was back in town, it would be selfish to keep them apart.

"Cade, hi."

I held the door open, gesturing for her to precede me. An eyebrow shot up as she searched my expression. I knew I looked pained; keeping my hands to myself was harder than I thought it would be. I wanted to hold her hand or put my hand on the small of her back. I would do anything to be able to touch her again. "After you."

"Thanks." Her heels clicked over the black and white tiled floor as she headed to what had been our favorite spot in the place. Nestled in the far corner, the circle booth was private, dimly lit by a single hanging light over the table, and romantic as hell. We used to slide close and share our food, whispering secrets, feeling each other up under the table, and eye-fucking until we could get back home to fuck for real. My god, how I had missed her.

I had avoided this spot since she left me, preferring to sit up at the bar, and I never brought a date here, ever. The subconscious reasons for my behavior hit me as a huge wave of memories almost swept me off my feet. I sat down hard on my side of the booth and dodged her eyes.

"I missed it here," she said, drawing my gaze.

"Yeah . . ." Looking at her was a mistake. Between the soft light and her even softer expression, I was done for. I had zero chance of this lunch ending with my heart intact. It had flown out of my chest the second I met her wistful eyes with mine.

"Charlotte! Oh my god! I've missed you so much."

"It's good to see you, Savannah, it's been too long." She slid out of the booth to hug my cousin and I took the opportunity to shove my napkin into my lap to cover up the evidence of my still-existing attraction to her.

Savannah was our age; we'd all gone to school together. The laws of small town living while in the same family dictated that she knew the entire history of my marriage to Charlotte.

"Welcome back to Sweetbriar! Sit down, girl. I bet I know what you want—burger with extra pickles on the side and tots, right?"

"Heck yes! But no beer. It's way too early. I'm still in the caffeination phase of my day so I'll take a Dr. Pepper."

"Don't forget the cheese on the tots," I added, flinching as the sharp point of Charlotte's boot poked my shin.

"Oh god." She placed her palm on my arm. "My foot slipped when I was scooting over. I'm so sorry, Cade."

Savannah laughed. "Would you like to try our new milkshake? We have a yummy hazelnut flavor that Oliver is trying out—lactose free." She gave me a pointed look and my eyes went wide. "You can try it on the house."

Oliver was another cousin. After my Uncle Pat died about ten years ago, running this place became a family affair. You could always find either my Aunt Delphine—Mom's sister—or any one of my cousins working behind the bar. Uncle Pat had recreated a piece of his home in Sweetbriar. Holloway's had all the charm of an Irish pub, right here on Main Street: cozy booths, dark wood, a big stone fireplace, family pictures on the walls, and a long bar that ran the entire rear of the building.

"A milkshake sounds awesome," Charlotte answered. "Thank you."

"I'll have the same thing. Plus, burger and tots."

"I know. Like you'd ever get anything different, Cade." She stepped back with a smile. "Some things never change no matter how much time has gone by. It's so great to see you both here, back in your booth, just like the old days." After another knowing grin she left to put our order in without ever taking out her notebook.

"Are you okay, Cade? You look—"

I forced my expression back to neutral. "I'm fine."

"*Gah!* Okay, I kicked you. I didn't mean to do it. Cheese is my weakness, and you know that it doesn't agree with me, Cade, jeez. I've felt awkward and strange since I came back to town. I'm freaking out, my deadline is approaching like a frickin' tsunami from hell, and there isn't enough caffeine or hours in the day left for me to finish on time. I have no excuse. I lost my cool. I'll pay for our lunch to make it up to you and your shin."

Without meaning to, I reached for her hands across the table, and with an equal lack of consideration, she took them, interlocking our fingers together exactly like we used to do. "Chill out. It wasn't a kick. It was barely even a nudge." My lips lifted in a half smile. "If I recall correctly, cheese agrees with you just fine."

She turned bright red and stared at the table. A soft gasp left her lips as she noticed our hands locked together, then withdrew hers from my grasp. "Do not say a word."

I chuckled. "You mean about the fart that will live forever in infamy? And the fact that cheese makes you flatulent?"

"Shh!" After a sweep around the restaurant to make sure no one heard, she turned to me. "Oh my god. Stop it!" she hissed. "I had to eat that mac and cheese, Caden, and I might regret it forever, but it was the first dinner you ever cooked for me in our own house, and I didn't want to hurt your feelings—"

"Or have me to find out that you're a human being who farts just like everybody else?"

She buried her face in her hands. "We were newly-weds. I wanted you to think I was dainty and cute."

"You are dainty and cute. In fact, you're fucking beautiful, and I can't believe it took becoming man and wife before you would fart in front of me, Charlotte."

Her head fell to her arms on the table as she groaned. "You cried, Cade."

"I didn't cry. I welled up, okay? It was a moment." I folded my jacket and placed it in the corner as an excuse to look away from her adorably overdramatic reaction. Charlotte could be over the top sometimes and I had always loved it.

"Let's talk about something else. Literally anything else. Please," she mumbled into her arm.

"You got it. What brought you back to Sweetbriar?" I decided to dive right into my questions. Small talk was pointless when you knew someone as well as we had known each other.

"Straight into the deep end." Her smiling eyes snapped to mine, and she laughed. "You haven't changed a bit."

I shrugged in answer, tapping my fingers on the table, stuck in the pale blue beauty of her gaze.

"I decided to finish writing my book here. And I missed my dad and brothers."

"That's it? You sure?"

Now she was the one to shrug in answer. It had never been this hard to get her to talk to me. It used to be the opposite; we'd lie in bed together, kissing, making love, talking for hours, sometimes until the sun came up. We'd always had something to say to each other.

I sighed as we drifted into another silence.

Savannah interrupted the quiet with our orders.

Charlotte snatched her milkshake from the table for a taste. "Oooooh, this is really good. Tell Oliver he's amazing as usual. Um, I'm doing Vi's next book club. You should come, Savannah." She grabbed a cheesy tot and ate it, shooting me a mock glare as she chewed.

"You know I never miss Vi's book club but talking about your books is going to be the best. Adaline is a total badass. Are you planning to hook her up with that new hot cop from the last book? What's his name? Jaden Skerrit?"

Her eyes darted to mine before she answered. "I haven't gotten far enough into my manuscript, so we'll all have to wait and see."

"I can't believe you killed her husband off—RIP, poor Tim! That was the one time I wished I'd read spoilers. When I got to that chapter, I cried my eyes out. You owe me a dang beer, Charlotte."

"*Gah!* I'm sorry. But I thought we were cool since you sent me that 'Tears of my Readers' coffee mug."

"Ha! I bet you drink out of it every morning and cackle maniacally, don't you?"

"I would never!" Charlotte gasped with mock offence as she steepled her fingers beneath her chin and let out a teasing evil laugh.

A ridiculous stab of jealousy hit me. She could talk and joke so easily with Savannah, or Elizabeth, even my mother, and Violet. But not with me.

"Well, you already know I can't wait for the next book. You guys enjoy your burgers," she said through a grin.

"Thank you, Savannah. It was so good to finally see you again."

"We missed you around here. Let me know if you need anything."

"Will do," I called to her retreating back before turning to face Charlotte. "So, Vi's book club, huh? Fair warning, there is book talk, but they mostly get tipsy and gossip, right?"

She lightly smacked a hand on the table and laughed. "That's the only reason why I agreed to do it. I can't talk about my books, here, in my hometown with people I grew up around, not with any kind of seriousness. I'd feel like a pretentious ass."

I drew my head back in surprise. "It's not pretentious to talk about your work. Everyone in town loves your books."

A lovely blush rose over her cheeks as she contemplated my statement. God, she was so damn cute. "Noooooo, no one reads them, just Savannah and Elizabeth," she scoffed. "People are just being nice because I grew up here."

I chuckled. "Sorry to break it to you but that isn't true. You have a lot of readers in town."

"Let's talk about something else. Adaline and I aren't getting along lately and I'm mad at her."

"Ah, she's not talking to you?" I took a bite of my burger and waited to see if I would get an answer or a shrug.

"Nope. She's unusually quiet. I'm getting kind of nervous about it, if I'm being honest. My deadline is looming over me like a nightmare."

"Call my mom," I suggested. "Write with her at Vi's. She swears it's the secret to her productivity—a constant flow of caffeine and baked goods while observing the good folk of Sweetbriar going about their daily business."

She bit her lip in indecision. "You wouldn't mind if I did that? Really? Are you sure?" The eagerness in her expression made me smile.

"Not at all."

"Thank you, Cade." She beamed at me. "I missed writing with your mom so much." She seemed to have missed everyone except for me.

Ouch.

Without meaning to, I rubbed a circle over my chest, to ease the ache there caused by her words—or rather, her lack of any words that would imply she had missed me too.

She was so cavalier about being gone, like it was no big deal. But it had devastated my life when she left and it was only in the last few years I had managed to pick up the pieces and put them back into some semblance of what I used to be.

"Of course. Just because you moved away doesn't mean this isn't your home."

"Right. Sweetbriar will always be home for me."

"And now you're back. You should feel comfortable here. I want you to."

The weight of her stare silenced me once more as my heart stuttered in my chest.

We spent the rest of lunch in companiable quiet. It was comfortable instead of awkward. Maybe this had been a good idea after all.

"I brought your check." Collectively startled by Savannah's voice, we both jumped, then drew our hands back sharply when we reached for the check at the same time. "You two will always be the cutest." She spun away, heading back toward the bar.

"Let me pay," Charlotte said.

"I invited you, remember?"

"Fine. But I'll get the next one. I really do need to get back to my laptop." She slid out of the booth then bent to retrieve her purse and jacket. She hesitated at the edge of the table. Her smile was sad, and maybe kind of longing too. I found myself wanting to ask her to stay, for coffee or dessert. Or to come home with me for dessert of a different kind, then coffee in the morning. "Thank you, Cade. I'm glad we did this," she finally said as she slipped into her jacket.

"I am too. Bye, Charlotte."

The next one. I took comfort in those words and smiled to myself as I dug in my pocket for my wallet. There would be a next one, I'd make sure of it.

I paid Savannah, then stopped in the doorway, squinting into the sun. Was someone taking pictures of Charlotte in her Jeep?

I jogged across the parking lot toward a man with a camera pointed at her, tracking her Jeep as she drove away. He appeared to be deliberately nondescript. Medium height and build, pale, with a baseball cap and a brown leather jacket. But his camera was expensive. He had to be a major photography buff or a professional.

"Hey, what are you up to?" I didn't identify myself as law enforcement even though I should have.

"Nothing. Just taking pictures. It's a free country."

"Yeah. It is. And there are hundreds of more interesting and picture worthy spots around here. Why would you choose a parking lot to photograph?"

"No reason. I'm new here. I'm still getting used to the area." He dodged my question.

"I'm Detective Caden Barrett, Sweetbriar PD, and it appeared that you were taking pictures of the Jeep that drove away. We don't take kindly to folks photographing people trying to go about their day. May I see your ID? And your camera please."

His friendly smile turned sly. "Am I being detained?"

I huffed a sigh. "No, you are not."

"Have I committed a crime?"

"I don't know yet. Have you?"

He smirked. "Since you obviously don't have a warrant for the camera, we both know I don't have to show you anything. I'll be on my way. Have a nice day, Detective Caden Barrett, Sweetbriar PD."

I narrowed my eyes, watching as he got into a rental car and drove off. Removing my cellphone, I took pictures and notated the license plate number and the make and model, then texted the info to my partner, Trevor, to run.

I couldn't put my finger on why his presence bothered me so much, not yet anyway. Charlotte was famous, and it was possible he was simply a fan. Or he could be telling the truth. One thing for certain though, I wouldn't wait for something to happen. I always trusted my gut; it hadn't led me wrong yet.

Minutes later, Trevor shot me a text. The rental was legit and the driver had a clean record; he was an attorney from Pennsylvania.

Chapter 6
Charlotte

As the great Taylor Swift had once kind of said: I knew he was trouble, yet I walked right into Holloway's anyway. I had pulled up in my Jeep to find him standing there, all long legs and broad shoulders, big biceps, and that glorious beard . . . The beard was new, and I liked it. *A lot.* Anyway, he was hotter than ever, and I was drifting into yearning, burning, crushing-on-Cade territory again. I was stuck in a middle school déjà vu; maybe I'd go home and cry into my journal over a juice box and some Cheetos.

The smart thing to do would be to steer clear of him. He was an irresistibly rugged, brawny mountain man cop now. I would bet money he could rip a log in half like Captain America. I would also pay good money to see him do it—shirtless, maybe even pantsless.

Be smart, Charlotte. Stay away.

I didn't want to be smart. Being smart was boring. What I wanted to do was find him and see how that sexy beard would feel running over every inch of my body. Would it tickle? I bet it would.

Why couldn't I?

Why shouldn't I?

We were consenting adults and we used to be so good together—*so freaking good . . .*

Argh! No more thinking about Cade's physical prowess allowed.

I had a career to maintain, one I had fought hard for. I had stuff, and things, and, vital, uh crap to do. Dang it, I couldn't afford to get wrapped up and distracted by a man. Not ever again.

I had goals. Big ones.

There were two things I had always wanted out of my life. From the time I first learned to read—when I saw all the magic contained within the pages of a book—I wanted to be a writer. And from the second I saw Caden Andrew Barrett walk through the door of the Sweetbriar Tiny Tots Preschool, carrying a blue teddy bear dressed like a cop and a Superman lunch box, I had known he would be mine someday. But during our senior year, I earned a full scholarship to NYU to study writing and that had turned my dream into a real-life, tangible goal—a goal I had been determined to reach.

But I couldn't have both. I'd tried it once, but stifling my dream and neglecting my goals had eaten me alive. I couldn't do it, not even for Cade. And I refused to hurt him ever again.

I'd married him after graduation, putting off college with the hope I could somehow convince him to come with me, or at least wait for me. I tried everything I could think of to keep both of my dreams in my life, but it wasn't meant to be—he had goals of his own that didn't mesh with mine.

I cut the engine and stared at my garage door. My landlord, old Mr. McMillon, known around town as a total cheapskate, had a bunch of crap stored in there, which was bullshit, but I had demanded a discount and got it, so I'd felt like I couldn't complain too much about having to park in the driveway. But who was I kidding? I could complain about anything, and I figured out real quick I would rather have a garage than a discount, especially when the weather was bad and I couldn't enter the house through the garage and my car was covered with freaking snow.

With a heavy sigh, I grabbed my stuff and hopped out to head for my front door. My townhouse was on the end of the row, with a front door facing a lovely side yard planted with evergreen shrubs and pine trees. It was the only one that didn't pick up the sound of traffic driving by. I was lucky to snag it despite the lack of garage space.

"Charlotte!" I spun, a huge smile chasing away my melancholy as my Sweetbriar-bestie Gwen came barreling out of her minivan to give me hugs and a welcome home present. "I hope it's okay to drop by. You've been here for what seems like forever, and I keep hearing from other people how great you look and all about what's going on with you. I had to see for myself."

"It's okay! I'm glad you're here! Can you come inside for a bit?"

"I can't stay long. I have to pick up the kids, otherwise I would drink all your coffee and force you to spill every detail of the lunch you just had with Cade."

"That's already going around town? Damn, I'm impressed."

"Don't tell me you forgot about the gossip mill in this town. I mean, Elizabeth and Mom are the main purveyors. I heard it from them." She passed me a gift bag.

I removed the tissue paper and pulled out a gorgeous windchime. "This is beautiful!"

She gestured to the empty plant hook extending from the beam by the porch railing. "Hang it right there and think of me every time it wakes you up at night."

I looped it over the hook. "It's perfect. Thanks Gwen."

"You're welcome! Love you, Charli."

"Love you too. We will catch up for real, over a long dinner with loads of wine before I go back to New York."

"No. I refuse to let you leave again. Next time I see you I'm bringing my marry-me-brownies. You'll stay in Sweetbriar, we can forget about men, buy a house together, and be roomies forever."

"God, I've missed you, you nerd, and you know I can't fight the power of your brownies. Dad and the brothers want me to stay too."

"And what about Cade?"

I shot her a look. "Don't even get that into your head. It's not going to happen."

"Why not? You loved each other so much—"

"And look how it ended. We broke each other's

hearts. We want different things from our lives. He wanted marriage, babies, a fricking dog. He wanted to stay here forever. His roots are planted so deep in Sweetbriar they'll never budge. You know that, Gwen, and you know me. I needed something more than that."

"Oh, Charli, that's not exactly true. Yeah, he's a Sweetbriar cop, just like he always wanted to become. But do you see a wife? No. Any kids running around? Also no. Not even a dog, Charlotte—nary a pet to be seen at Detective Caden Barrett's abode. Which just so happens to be the house you two lived in together while you were married, in case you forgot that pertinent fact."

I bit my lip and looked away rather than answering. I didn't want to get my hopes up or restart the pining, yearning, burning, and regretful feels that I had supposedly let go of.

"Look, Charlotte, I'm not saying he's been celibate all these years. He wasn't, and neither were you, for that matter. But no one got into his heart like you did and the same goes for you. That still means something, I just know it. And now I have to go pick up my kids, dang it." She pulled me in for a hug. "I miss your face. Think about what I said, please?"

"Okay. I'll think about it." I pulled away with a smile. "And rethink, and obsess, and freak out over it. You've met me, Gwen. You know how I do things."

"I miss you constantly." She opened her car door, then shouted at me over the roof. "You're my best friend in the world, Charli. I want you to stay. Adventures can be had close to home, and you know it's true!"

I waved as she pulled away from the curb and took off down the street. Everything Gwen said was the truth, but what she didn't know I'd been pouring over every detail of my marriage ever since I lifted myself off the snowy ground and saw Cade again. This shit kept me up at night. Did he still have feelings for me? Could it be true? Or was he simply trying to solve the mysterious case of why I lied when my car crashed into our tree?

Unearthing my key from the dark abyss of my purse, I let myself inside and headed for the kitchen to put my trashy groceries away and get a drink.

I couldn't get Cade and his elusive opinion of me out of my mind. I was also stewing over what it would be like to just stay here after I finished my book. New York was busy, crowded, loud, and the home of my dumbass stalker. Year by year I was slowly getting tired of living there. I felt truly safe for the first time in ages here in Sweetbriar; did I really want that feeling to end?

My laptop was on the counter, but I could have sworn I had left it charging in my room. All this stress was making me lose my dang mind. Nothing was ever where I'd thought I left it, damn it. I grabbed the laptop and a Diet Dr. Pepper and made my way to the couch to work.

I kicked off my boots and wiggled out of my jeans. Writing with pants on was impossible. Pants were the enemy of my creativity, along with bras—and deadlines. I heaved out a sigh and opened my computer, settling back into the cushions while I tried to open my mind to let the words start flowing.

My cell *pinged* with a text.

Shamefully, I closed the laptop and let it flop to the side as I scrambled to reach the phone on the coffee table. I was totally willing to get distracted. Shame on me. My work ethic had turned to crap over the last couple weeks.

Violet: Can I give Cade your number?

What the fudge?

I stood up, looking around my living room as if my décor had answers to why in the heck he wanted to contact me. My girly parts wanted him to want me, while my boring brain shouted that he just wanted answers about the crash.

Me: What for?

Violet: He wants to talk to you, silly. Don't forget about book club next week!

Me: I won't forget. And yes, give him my number.

I stared at the screen, waiting for it to light up with a call, or ping with a text. My heart expanded with anticipatory glee while my stupid weak knees shook. If I hadn't suspected I had residual feelings for Cade before, I sure as hell suspected it now. My body was going insane as I stood there grinning like a fool. Angels were singing, misty rainbows tickled my bare legs, and cloud nine was about to become my second home. *Gah!* I was floating on air as I waited for him to contact me.

And yet, the frickin' phone remained silent. I stared harder, trying to will a notification into existence.

Damn it, I was such an idiot. He'd asked for my number; that didn't mean he would call *immediately*.

And why was I flipping out over this?

We were divorced for eff's sake. He was my ex-husband for a reason.

I was out of practice. My fake marriage to New York-bestie-Trent had taken me off the market for a long time, and it had been well over a year since I'd had a date. And I wasn't exactly a player before my fake marriage. My game was seriously lacking, my experience was completely limited, and my heart was about to be smashed to pieces by Cade—again—because I never learned.

Ping!

"Ahhh!" My stomach shot to my feet and swirled back into place along with a burst of tingles. I tried to swipe to answer the text, but my trembling hands fumbled the phone, sending it tumbling to the couch.

"Oh crap, oh crap, oh crap." I picked it up, frowning at the screen when I saw it was one of my brothers—Hunter, number one, the scary one—demanding that I attend dinner tonight at the house to "talk over a few things."

Without bothering to text back, I called him. Yelling

at someone would be great for my stress levels. Lucky Hunter. "What do you want, Hunter?"

His tone was accusatory when he hissed out, "You went to lunch with Cade today."

"And that's your business, how?" My hand hit my hip as I prepared to go off.

"I'm your brother. He hurt you once and I won't let him do it again. That's how."

His kindness toward me and the implied threat against Cade took the edge off my annoyance, and I sighed. "I hurt him first. You know it's true."

"I might eventually concede that it was a tie and you hurt each other, but I'm still debating it. Come to the house for dinner at five o'clock. Dad's grilling out back. We'll talk about it when you get here." He hung up.

They were all nosy.

Intrusive, every single one of them.

And let's not forget bossy.

But I'd missed them, and my dad kicked ass on the grill, so I decided to forget how much I hated being ordered around and headed over there.

* * *

I was sitting on the covered back porch, wrapped in a quilt in front of the fire pit watching my dad and brothers cook a mountain of rib-eyes. It had started pouring rain and was now freezing cold, but nothing stopped them when they were in the mood to grill. They just threw up the portable tarp, lit up the fire pits, and went for it. Brody was prepping baked potatoes with all the fixings, Spencer was making a banana pudding, and Deacon's sun tea was struggling for life on the edge of the porch. We were in Oregon; sun tea was always an iffy beverage to attempt. As the saying went, if you don't like the weather in Oregon, wait five minutes. I mean, right now it was supposedly spring, for eff's sake.

I was glad I was here. Being alone in the mood I was in would have been terrible. "Hey, can one of you text me real quick?" I shouted. "I need to see something. My phone might be messed up."

Suddenly five texts blew up my phone and I smiled. "Thanks guys." Also, boooo! My phone was fine, and Cade hadn't called, texted, or FaceTimed me.

This was bullcrap.

I had definitely time traveled back to middle school, but this time there was no Sadie Hawkins Day dance I could use to force a reaction out of him. Cade used to be shy. He didn't strike me as shy anymore, but who knew? I hadn't been around for the last decade or so to see all the changes in him for myself.

I'd lost my mind. I needed a nap or an intervention—a Cadenvention. "I need a drink." I got up to head to the kitchen for a beer. Maybe I should go to my old room and mope. Perhaps throwing myself on my bed to cry it out like the old days would be therapeutic.

"How're you doing?"

I peeped around the door of the fridge. It was Tucker —number three, recently divorced and still nursing a broken heart. He'd moved back to the house a few months ago. "I should be asking how you are."

"I'm fine."

"Sure you are. Want a beer? Want to go hang out in my room with me? Maybe play an old Evanesence CD and cry a little bit."

He lifted his chin and held his hand out for a beer. "Cry? Over Cade? Yeah, he's a cop, but say the word and one of us will be happy to fuck him up a little bit."

"I meant cry over Sierra and the kids so I can comfort you, dork, and please don't fuck him up. I will admit the Cade situation is surprisingly stressful. But mainly I'm stressing because my deadline is too close for comfort and I'm beginning to think I have writer's block. Adaline and I aren't getting along." I didn't mention my stalker, good old Douggie W. McPsychopants. I still wasn't ready to talk about that, with anyone.

"How was your lunch date?"

I laughed. "Nice deflecting, Tucker. And please don't call it a date. Does anyone *not* know about it?"

He sipped his beer and pretended to think about it before shaking his head with a grin. "Nope."

"I figured. Even if this town is filled with busy bodies, I've missed it."

"That's a sign to stay, you know."

"Hmm, I don't know. Moving is hard and I—" My phone rang causing me to almost jump out of my skin. I glanced at the screen, "Holy crap, it's Cade. What do I do?"

Tucker's side-eye was legendary. "Try answering it for a start. Go to your room, talk it out." He took the bottle of beer from my hand, twisted the cap off for me and pointed me down the hall. "I'll keep everyone away and save you a plate."

"Thanks. I don't know what my problem is."

His eyes were sad when they met mine. "Good luck, Charli. Follow your heart."

"Love you, Tuck."

"Love you too. Go." *Answer the phone,* he mouthed.

After running down the hall and shutting myself into my old room I swiped to answer. "Hello?"

Chapter 7
Cade

Even though I knew I'd regret it, I called her. With no plan in mind, no goal, just winging it like a man who lived his life with no fear of rejection.

I paced my living room as it rang, almost giving up before I heard a frantic, "Hello?"

"Charlotte, you're breathless. Is everything okay?"

"Uh, yeah. I'm at my dad's place, in my old room." A nervous giggle escaped. "That's weird, right?"

Nostalgia washed over me. "Not at all. It's just like old times." I could picture her lounging on her canopied bed, on her side facing me as we 'studied' together after school. Her soft voice had always made my spine tingle. I had to see her again and not just randomly around town. I needed concrete plans and a guarantee.

Her voice startled me out of my longing thoughts. "We used to talk all night on the phone and be so tired at school the next day. Remember when I fell asleep in Mr. Nolan's class?"

"Charlotte. Have dinner with me. Please?"

"What? You're full of surprises, aren't you? And why? Do you want to question me about the accident some more?" Suspicion laced with a hint of teasing colored her tone.

Guilt charged through me. I wanted to help her, to talk to her, to have her trust me again. "What if I promise not to question you? Would that influence your answer?" Could I find out what I needed to know without driving her away?

"Probably, but I'm at my dad's. I can't tonight."

I laughed, feeling a bit sheepish. "Not tonight, I have better manners than that. And I know better than to suggest tomorrow night, but I'm doing it anyway despite the short notice. I have to see you. Come to my place? Seven?"

"Okay, you've convinced me. I'll be there. Can I bring anything?"

"We both know you can't cook," I teased.

"I'll bring my famous brownies for dessert. We both know how much you love them."

"Perfect." Her famous brownies were Gwen's creation, but I had never let on that I knew she was really the one who had always baked them. "Guess what? I'm in my old room too. But now it's a craft room that my mother never uses."

"That's right, it's Sunday. Do you guys still have the illustrious Barrett family Sunday dinner?"

"Yep, Mom has a fit if one of us misses it."

"I love that. Dad is the same way with his barbeques. I missed so many of them. Too many."

"It's been hailing off and on for the last hour. In fact, it might snow tonight. Is he out back grilling?" I asked with a laugh. "Under that beat up old tarp?"

"You know it. Rib-eyes are on the grill as we speak. All the brothers are contributing. Well, except for Tucker. He's getting spoiled today because his divorce is final now. And they don't let me cook anymore. The fire in the oven last time I visited was the final nail in that coffin."

"Except for the famous brownies, right?" I teased.

"Uh, yeah of course. The brownies—which I will bring to your house tomorrow night. Seven sharp."

"Perfect. We can watch a movie, or on the off chance it's a nice evening, we can eat on the deck and look at the stars."

"I remember looking at the stars with you." Her voice was barely a whisper in my ear.

My return whisper was a confession in hers. "I remember everything."

"Cade..."

"God, Charlotte, I know—" A knock at the door interrupted what was about to be a foolish, early declaration. Of what, I wasn't quite sure.

"Must be time for dinner. Tell everyone hi for me." Her soft laugh made me smile.

"Yeah, it is. Tomorrow, Charlotte."

"Yes. I'll see you at seven."

"I'll be waiting." I ended the call, my heart heavy with the realization that I had been waiting years for her and if I messed this opportunity up, I'd probably be waiting for her forever.

I opened the door to end up face to face with my sisters. Violet, my older sister, and my three younger sisters—identical twins Lily and Rose, and Holly, the baby. My brothers were at the house for dinner too, but they weren't quite as nosy as the girls and were busy watching TV with my dad in the living room.

"We're here for information," Rose, clearly the ringleader, demanded. No preamble, no easing in, straight to the point. She had settled down with my partner, Trevor, a couple months back. They were married, she was the stepmom to his kids, and they were all happy as a could be. In other words, she was in prime matchmaking form, and I had better be on my guard.

My mother said she was staying out of my business with Charlotte and—stupidly—her declaration had lulled me into a false sense of security. My four sisters all up in my face right now proved that I had plenty of intrusive questions headed my way.

"Yeah, spill your guts, Cade. Are you and Charlotte dating again?" Lily, her identical twin, asked. Not surprising, as those two always backed each other up.

"I brought you a Coke, here." Holly, my baby sister, passed me an icy tumbler then turned to take a seat on the sectional couch in the middle of the small central lounge area that the upstairs bedrooms surrounded. She flicked on the TV and pointedly started watching—owning her obvious role as "good cop."

"I'm just here to observe." Violet shrugged. "Or maybe referee?" She laughed as she joined Holly on the couch.

"No, we're not dating." I scooted around the twins, which wasn't hard since they were tiny, and headed for the stairs.

"Oh, come on. Sit with us." Holly said with a laugh. "You can watch ESPN with Dad anytime. We're all in the mood to offer high quality advice. You want her back, don't you?"

I stopped, hand on the banister as I considered their offer. "Maybe." That was all I was willing to admit at this point.

Violet's chuckle made me turn around. "We know you do. Let us help."

"We're not going to get all pushy and intrusive, I promise. I came on too strong before." Lily was sheepish. "We just want to talk to you. We all love Charlotte. You used to make each other so happy."

"I'm totally going to be pushy and intrusive," Rose scoffed. "You need her back in your life. You haven't been the same since she left. And I have an ace in the hole too. Trevor is your partner—"

"Yeah, and that's a sacred bond, Rose." I argued. "He's not going to turn into your matchmaking minion. Where is he anyway?"

"Downstairs somewhere. And of course, it's sacred. I

only meant that he wants you to be happy just as much as I do."

"Okay, but now we're dropping this topic."

"Also, Trevor is smart. He'll give you good advice. When the time comes, you should listen to it."

"Who says I'll need advice? Is it time for dinner yet?"

"Cade! You haven't dated anyone seriously since Charlotte—"

"I've had girlfriends, Rose—"

"But—"

"Ten minutes," Holly answered. "Until dinner."

"Thank you, Holly."

"You're welcome. Mom said to leave you alone and I'm not in the mood to badger you with questions. I just got back to town and I'm staying for good. I want to settle into Sunday dinners and family time. It's time for me to take it easy, you know?" Holly had just shut down her travel blog and moved back to town permanently. But I wasn't sure if she was messing with me or not. She used to tell everybody she wanted to be a private detective like Nancy Drew. She'd follow me and my older brother, Asher, everywhere when we were kids and wrote down everything we did in a little flip notebook, like we were a case she was working on. Holly had been an interesting kid.

"All right . . ." I studied her earnest face with suspicion. My sisters always wanted to know my business, except Violet. But I usually ended up confiding everything to her on my own. And to her credit she had kept everything I'd ever told her about my relationship with Charlotte to herself.

"You have your cop face on, Cade." Violet laughed and patted the cushion next to her for me to sit down.

"Can you blame me?" It felt like a trap; her smile was innocent, but I knew her intentions were not. If I sat down, I'd end up spilling my guts and I didn't want anyone else to know how I was feeling about Charlotte. If things didn't work out again it would be humiliating.

"I don't blame you," Rose answered. "I'd be scared of all of us put together too."

"Well. Um . . ." I stalled, waiting, and hoped my mother would yell that dinner was ready so I could go downstairs and not hurt anyone's feelings. I sipped my Coke and lingered at the head of the staircase.

"Five minutes," Holly announced, her green eyes gleaming with faux innocence. Maybe now that she wasn't out and about and traveling anymore, she wanted to start that detective crap up again. Or maybe now I was getting paranoid we were actual adults, for fuck's sake.

"Dinner is almost on the table!" Our mother's shout interrupted all the awkwardness that was about to mortify me. "Come on down!"

"Thank god." I all but ran down the stairs, soda sloshing around in my glass and laughter trailing behind me as I descended.

I stopped in the living room and sat on the couch. Sipping my Coke, I contemplated choosing one of them to talk to. I was leaning toward Violet when Rose joined me on the couch.

"Sorry about that. I get carried away sometimes."

"It's okay, I know you can't help yourself," I teased.

"Yeah, yeah, make your fun. But I feel like I owe you, Cade. You have no idea how much you helped me back when Trevor and I were messing everything up with each other."

"Really? I did?"

"Yeah, remember after Trevor got shot? You said I should just sit with my feelings and let them sink in so I could work through them. I think that's what you should do now. You've been trying to forget about Charlotte for years and you two avoided each other every time she came to town to see her family. Things are different this time. It has to be a big adjustment. It must still hurt."

I looked at her from the corner of my eye. "Thanks." I wasn't ready to admit to anyone how much my heart hurt whenever I saw her. How I wanted to take her in my arms and kiss her or just simply talk to her and be at ease with her like I used to, in a way I took for granted for so many years.

"Of course. And I'm not going to butt in, I promise."

I scoffed. "I'm not counting on that."

"No, I mean, I'm not going to try and set you two up or meddle in your business, nothing like that. I will, however, always get nosy and ask you stuff. I can't, like, completely change my personality. But no games. I swear."

"Now, that feels more realistic."

"See? Growth and change. Sitting with your feelings, talking things through, all that stuff is smart. You should do it with this situation. I do it all the time now and I feel like a total adult. Trevor and I are kicking so much marriage ass."

"I'm happy for you two, and I'll try it." I already felt myself pushing half of her good advice to the back of my mind and even though I knew it was a bad idea to deny what I was feeling for Charlotte, I was doing it anyway.

Clearing her throat to interrupt us, Mom came up behind the couch and shot a pointed look at my sister. "We talked about this, Rose." Rose raised her hands in silent defense and my mother turned to me. "I'm here to rescue you, Cade. Go in the dining room with your brothers."

"She's fine, Mom." Her eyebrows raised in disbelief, and I laughed. "She's offering quality life advice now, so no worries. Thank you, Rose."

Rose laughed then stuck her tongue out. "See, Mother? I know how to keep a promise."

"Then I apologize, sweetheart. Go on up and get your sisters for dinner."

I followed Mom through the arched entrance to the dining room while Rose went upstairs. "Go on and sit down." She waved me toward the table before bustling back to the kitchen.

I took the seat between Levi and Jude—fraternal twins, the babies of the family, and always first to the table. In fact, they crashed in their old rooms pretty often. Neither one of them were fond of cooking and my mother still loved to baby them.

"How's Charlotte doing?" Levi asked and I groaned.

"Not you too. Enough."

"Ooh, touchy." Jude chuckled. "Must be serious."

"Zip it or I'll ask you about Harper when the girls get down here." Harper was his best friend since childhood and eventually they would be more. Everyone knew it but the two of them.

"Fine." He sipped his drink. "Consider it zipped. That's a can of worms I don't want opened in front of them."

Levi laughed and took a swig of his beer.

I shot him a glare. "I don't know why you think this is funny."

Jude smirked then cleared his throat, but it sounded more like the name "Becca" than an actual cough.

"Fine, Cade, I have your back too. No Charlotte talk tonight as long as you don't bring *her* up again." Becca was the living embodiment of the word *regret* for Levi and had been for years. He had messed up his relationship with her almost every way a man could screw up with a woman aside from cheating. The only thing he had left going for him was his loyalty. I had my doubts about the two of them ever working it out. But, on the other hand, I never imagined Charlotte would ever come back to Sweetbriar, yet here I sat with hope forming in my heart and dinner plans with her tomorrow confirmed.

Trevor entered the room, carrying a beer. "I need to talk to you." I gestured for him to follow me out to the patio.

"What's up?"

"Have you found out anything more about Charlotte's accident? I'm beginning to think she might be telling the truth about not being followed."

"Nothing." He shook his head and sipped his beer. "If she suspected someone aside from Bethany was following her, she's keeping that secret close to the vest. There is no other way to know where to start looking since I couldn't find anyone who saw anything out of the ordinary that day to give me something to go on."

"I couldn't either. And the parking lot photographer was a no-go as well. He checks out. I took a deeper look and found nothing hidden. He's not even from New York."

"Maybe drop it for now? And keep our eyes and ears open for anything that might come up."

"Yeah, I—"

"Want to get to know her again? Be part of her life again? Get in her pants again? Maybe marry her again someday?" He laughed. "I know, Rose has mentioned it once or twice." His smile was knowing, but unlike almost everyone else in my family, he wouldn't pry or tease, and meddling was the last thing he would ever do.

"Thanks for not giving me shit about this."

"They just want you to be happy."

"I know. Still, I appreciate being able to talk to you without getting the third degree."

"Always, man."

Dinner went by as it did every Sunday, full of laughter and food and maybe a few minor arguments.

The topic of me and Charlotte had been successfully avoided, probably because Mom had taken herself out of the equation. Plus, I had effectively threatened Levi and Jude such that they deflected all attempts to ask about her every time anyone tried to bring her up.

Chapter 8
Charlotte

"Tomorrow at seven" had come real quick.

I stared at my face in the mirror. Dinner, with Cade. A freaking *date* with my ex-husband. What the fudge had I been thinking?

The time was nigh. I took a deep, cleansing breath and stepped away from the mirror.

I had to get going or I'd be late. Self-reflection and contemplation were good things, but I was bordering on ridiculous and my anxiety levels were headed for the roof.

This was supposed to be no big deal. Just a simple dinner between exes. I needed an outfit that said "*Yes, I will bang you*" without being too obvious. It had to be sexy but not overt. Welcoming but not easy. I should wear a dress or a skirt. Or maybe I should wear something casual, like a soft oversized sweater and some leggings.

What does one wear when they were hoping to—? *What exactly was I hoping for?* My feelings for Cade were nothing but a jumble of confusing thoughts rambling around in my head. I mean, I wanted this dinner to be a real date with a real chance of getting back into his bed, but was that all I wanted? Did I want to get back into his heart too? Maybe be part of his life again? *Yes, you do, you stupid, stupid, obsessive little Cade-obsessed freakshow.*

Why did I do this to myself? I lived my life disconnected with reality. My heart was never in sync with my brain. I spent my time avoiding my feelings and not examining my desires until I didn't know how I truly felt about anything, and then I couldn't understand why I was hurting all the time. It always took me forever to figure myself out and determining what I wanted was impossible. Right now, I was wondering if I was actually pathetic enough to have a crush on my ex-husband. It would definitely be on-brand for me.

Frustrated, I studied my reflection.

All the components for a hot night were there.

Matching undies: check

Flawless makeup and good hair: check

Fresh bikini wax: check

What was I missing? Oh yeah, I lacked clarity and probably the ability to make good life choices. *Ugh!*

After coming to zero conclusions about my true motivation, I turned away from the mirror and grabbed a pair of black leggings and an oversized cashmere sweater in Cade's favorite shade of blue from the pile on the floor and put them on. I might as well be comfortable in a situation that had plenty of potential to get uncomfortable. I found my boots and purse, slipped into my coat, and headed out for Cade's place. Gwen had been nice enough to drop off her welcome home Marry-Me Brownies, so I was good to go.

It had dumped snow all night so the drive up to his place was precarious and took forever, but since I grew up here, I did just fine. I only crashed the other day because I was out of my damn mind with fear and forced to go too fast. I knew these roads like the back of my hand; after all, this used to be my house, too.

The Ponderosa pine stood like a sentry guarding the turn-off that led up to Cade's property. I remembered back when we chose this place. The house was rundown, in need of a lot of repairs. Cade's dad, Ben, who was not only the Chief of the Sweetbriar Police Department but also a major home renovation addict, encouraged us to take it. With his help, Cade and I transformed our little house into a three-bedroom, two-bathroom home, cozy and cute. Perfect for starting the family Cade was so eager to have. I wanted a family too, but I wanted other things first.

Why is it okay for men to do things while women get to be things? Why is it acceptable for a man to be a husband and a father while also chasing his goals and ambitions? Whereas I was the bad guy for wanting more? I could be pretty and sweet, a wife and a mom, and that was fine and good—*yay Charlotte*. But the second I wanted to do something else along with it, like write books or have a career then it's all about how no one can have it all . . .

I shook my head. I'd made my choice. Living with it sucked sometimes, but I wouldn't change anything.

Why hadn't he found someone else to help him build the life he had wished for? He had been so adamant about what he needed for his future. He wanted to be married young, have kids right away, and serve Sweetbriar while working toward taking over as Chief of Police from his dad.

Cade was a good man. He was sweet and romantic. Loving and kind. The type of man any woman would be lucky to have. But none of his dreams had come true. He lived here alone. I pulled up into the driveway and came to a stop. He had shoveled the walkway, making it easy for me to get to the front door. I added considerate to the list of qualities that made Cade a catch.

My boots crunched over the path toward the porch. Time seemed to go backward with every step I took. I remembered days when I'd come home from work, and how if Cade was off or had an early shift, he would always cook dinner. We'd eat together, talking about life, and our days, and our plans for the future. But the hope that he'd reconsider and go with me to New York so I could use my scholarship had always been in the back of my mind.

My mood changed from excitement to something I'd never felt before. I wished I were standing here under different circumstances. I didn't regret my choices; I just wished I never had to make them.

I knocked and held my breath as his footsteps grew

closer to the door, and exhaled in an anxious rush as he opened it.

His eyes roved greedily over me, like I was his dinner instead of whatever he had cooking inside. "I can't quite believe you're here. Finally." He wore jeans and a long-sleeved black Henley, rolled up at his forearms and snug around his biceps and chest. His feet were bare, but the house was warm. I could feel it from where I stood. "Come on inside. You look beautiful, Charlotte."

"Well, I'd better," I joked. "All my clothes are on the floor of my bedroom. I tried on everything I own. I was so nervous." He helped me out of my coat and took the brownies from my hand with a wink.

He took in my sweater and leggings; a grin raised his lips up at one corner as he closed the door. "You chose well. That sweater matches your eyes. So pretty."

"Thank you." A nervous giggle escaped despite my best efforts to appear unaffected. "You're gorgeous as usual."

He waved a hand with a chuckle. "What? In this old thing?"

"God, Cade. This feels—"

"Almost like old times, I know."

"I can't believe I'm here again . . ." I stepped further into the living room. "The place looks great."

"I got some new furniture, fixed up the backyard and deck a bit—"

"It smells wonderful." I crossed to the kitchen and set my purse next to where he'd placed the brownies on the counter. "What have you done in here? It looks awesome." He had remodeled the kitchen and whatever he was cooking had me drooling. Or was it his sexy self that had me salivating? I couldn't make up my mind, seeing as how I was trying not to stare at him too hard and make a fool of myself.

He came up behind me, putting a warm hand on my waist as he stood at my back and pointed out what he had done. "Dad and I gutted the entire space and did it all ourselves. Marble counters, the cabinets are all custom, and the wood flooring goes throughout the entire house now."

I turned to face him, but he didn't remove his hand; instead he let it drift around to the small of my back to gently tug me closer. "Of course, your dad would never hear of hiring a contractor, not when he's so good at remodels."

His eyes were hot on mine. "Yeah, let's talk about the kitchen later. Charli baby, come here."

I knew this look on his face.

I freaking loved this look.

"I'm right here, Cade." If he didn't kiss me, I would die. Suddenly his lips on mine were the only thing in the entire world I wanted to feel.

"Meet me halfway," he murmured, his voice dark and husky. "I need to know you want it too."

My lips parted and I hesitated half a second before taking a step into the solid warmth of his body. My breasts brushed his chest, and I shivered at the familiar contact as he drew me closer and his head dropped infinitesimally closer to mine.

God, I loved his lips. They could be soft and hard at the same time, and he knew how to make me feel good everywhere. Jeez, how would the beard feel? I reached up to encircle his neck with my arms, letting my fingers drift into his hair. I whispered my admission. "I want you too." My eyes darted from his to his lips and back up again. "Kiss me, please."

"I missed you." His words were almost lost in the air between us as his mouth pressed against mine, closing what was left of the distance.

I let out a whimper and pushed closer, seeking more of the hard force of his body. *This is what I'd been missing in my life.* All other thoughts left my head as he kissed me and I lost myself in his arms. Past and present collided as his tongue slid against mine, claiming me in a way no one else ever could. No matter how badly I had wanted to forget what it felt like to kiss Cade, he'd always been there in the back of my mind whenever I'd kissed someone else.

He stepped into me, leg between mine, hands at my waist, and backed me up until my hips nestled into the corner of the counter. I stood, breathless, caged in by him, by his insistent gaze, greedy mouth, and seeking hands. "I've been dying to kiss you since you crashed into our tree." His growl against my lips sent a shudder through me. All I could do was hang on tight, gripping his strong forearm with a desperate clasp of my trembling hand.

"Cade . . ." I gasped before his lips took mine again. That beard I was so curious about tickled my chin and cheeks as our kiss became frantic. His body was hard against mine, chest like a wall, strong arms banded around me like he'd never let me go.

I tried to keep up with the kiss, to give to him what he was giving to me, but I couldn't. He was too much, too strong, too overwhelming. I gave up and let him give us both what we needed.

This kiss told me more about the changes in him than any of our other interactions since I got back to Sweetbriar had. This Cade was dominant and determined, he wanted me, and he was going to take what he wanted.

His innate sweetness was now wrapped up with something forceful and primal. He was utterly intoxicating, and I wanted to know everything I'd missed out on. His hands drifted down to my ass, kneading into my flesh as he ground himself against me.

It was pent-up, furious, and beyond anything we had ever shared together. We were rapidly spinning out of control, and I didn't want to stop.

"Yes, Cade, yes." I breathed as I ran my palms down the hard planes of his chest to grip his shirt in my hands and haul him closer.

Ding! Ding! Ding!

Slowly I forced my eyes open. The timer on his stove was going off but he didn't notice. His eyes were still closed; he was seemingly unaware of anything but me and him. His broad palm moved to my jaw, cupping my chin, fingers pressing into my cheek as he deepened our kiss.

My eyes slammed shut again.

Screw dinner.

Ding! Ding! Ding!

I drew my head back. "Cade—"

His eyes blazed into mine. "Damn, Charlotte."

"That was . . ." *Amazing and probably life altering.*

He took in a shaky breath before smiling at me. "I promised you dinner, didn't I?" With a reach behind himself, he shut off the timer.

"Oh yeah . . . dinner." I swayed, off balance at the sudden loss of his lips on mine. But slowing things down was probably a good idea. I hadn't expected to walk into his kitchen and straight into the fire.

"Go sit on the couch, baby. I'll bring you a plate."

Finally coming back to my senses, I teased him to lighten the heavy mood we had stumbled into. "I hope it's not mac and cheese."

"I know better," he teased back.

"Can I help?"

"Sure. Grab the wine and glasses. In the cupboard—"

"Above the fridge, right?" I raised an eyebrow.

His lips tilted to the side in a grin as he nodded.

"The kitchen may be a little different, but your organizational skills are still the same."

"Old habits die hard, I guess." He bent and removed a casserole dish from the oven and set it on the stove. "So, I made lemon chicken. I know it's basic, but I think I've finally perfected the recipe." He was sheepish as he stuck a bag of rice into the microwave. "I have not yet perfected rice, however."

"Hey, microwave rice is one of my staples, along with Marie Calendar meals and canned soup. I'm not gonna judge it. I haven't perfected anything except ordering take-out. Pizza is my specialty." I grabbed a bottle of red, the wine bottle opener, and two glasses and made my way to the living room. I kicked off my boots and sat on the couch, tucking my legs beneath me.

Even though it was different here and we had both changed so much, it still felt like I was home, like I'd never left. It was almost as if the years hadn't crept between us, and we were back where we once were. Tears filled my eyes, with a sharp inhale I brushed them away and attempted to regain control of my emotions. Every part of my being had suddenly become desperate to make this work with him. My heart was a twisted mess of anticipation in my chest as I poured the wine and waited for him. I had no idea what would happen next; it was terrifying and exhilarating all at the same time.

Chill out, Charlotte. I poured a glass of wine and attempted to relax.

He entered, set our plates on the coffee table, then froze as he sat down. "I'm sorry," he blurted.

Surprised, I turned to him with my glass of wine halfway to my mouth. "For what?"

"Uh, I didn't set the table. I didn't put out candles or flowers." His head hung. "What was I thinking? I just served you at the coffee table like it was ten years ago. Shit, I should have taken you to the Riverview Grille or someplace nice—"

"Stop. I love it, I swear. This is comfortable and cozy and I'm so happy I feel this way with you right now. Please don't be sorry, Cade."

"You don't think I'm a tool for not taking you out on a real date?"

"I swear I don't. This is perfect. I love it, Cade. We're far beyond dating anyway. I mean, look at me. I'm not wearing shoes, my feet are up, and you even have my favorite wine. I'm good. I love everything, I promise you."

Relief suffused his features. "Okay, I believe you, but next time we're getting fancy at the Riverview and I'm buying. Now, taste the chicken and tell me what you think." He cut a piece from my plate and held it aloft to feed me.

I opened my mouth to take the bite, then shut it with a giggle. "This is funny."

His mock frown made me laugh harder. "Take a bite or I will turn this fork into an airplane and fly the chicken into your mouth like I do for Calla." Calla was his niece. His younger sister Lily was her mom. I'd met her at Violet's a few weeks ago, and though she was adorable, it had made me sad. Because if I were still married to Cade, I'd be her aunt.

"Not gonna lie, I kinda want to see you do the airplane noises. I will also accept *choo choo* and *vroom*."

Now he was laughing too. "Try it. I'm a much better cook than when we were toge—never mind."

I opened my mouth and he popped it in. My eyebrows went up. It was great. I covered my mouth with a hand as I nodded my approval. "It's delicious. Tarragon?"

"Yep, it's Gram's recipe."

"I never tried this one." I used to go to their Sunday

dinners all the time and had probably tasted most of their family specialties. "How is she? I haven't seen her yet."

"She's good. She lives in the apartment above the garage now. Rose is married to my partner, Trevor, and they live in Gram's house with his kids. You'll have to come to the next Sunday dinner."

A thrill shot through me at the thought of going to his parent's house with him, but I decided not to think too hard about it for now or I would get carried away. "Rose is the only one of your sisters I haven't seen in town yet. You already know that I've relapsed and am addicted to Violet's coffee again, so we see each other all the time. And Holly and I ran the track at the high school together the other day. It was nice to catch up with her." Part of what I missed when Cade and I split up was his sisters. They were awesome and had always treated me like I was one of them.

"She's finished with her travel blog—she shut it down. Did she tell you? She's staying in Sweetbriar now, just like you."

I froze. I had thought of staying in town, that was true. But I hadn't made a one-hundred-percent definite decision yet. "Uh—"

"Do you want to see what's on TV and make this evening historically accurate?" His eyes twinkled as he sipped his wine.

"Let's do it." We could talk about my future non-plans and uncertainty later. Reality could wait. This was fun and I didn't want to ruin it.

He powered it up, and the news was on. Trent was

being interviewed about his new play for an entertainment segment. "Oh crap."

This was just great; my second ex-husband was on the television while I sat eating dinner with my first ex-husband.

"Well, this isn't awkward at all," he quipped.

"Um . . ."

*"You're recently divorced from the best-selling author of the **Adaline Paige Mysteries**, Keli Marlowe. What happened, Trent? How are you holding up?"*

"Keli will always be my best friend. Look, we got married on a whim. We were lonely. We were never meant to be man and wife. In fact, she'll be back home right here in New York as soon as the latest Adaline mystery is done. We'll have our usual celebratory lobster dinner and toast to another best seller. I'm fine, she's fine. Everything is fine."

Trent's laughter rang out from the speakers, and I flinched, afraid to look at Cade and see his reaction. As far as Trent knew, that was my plan; he wasn't lying. I hadn't spoken to him about Cade, so he had no clue I had been considering staying in Sweetbriar.

Chapter 9
Cade

She's leaving?

I'm such an idiot.

I let my heart get in front of my logic with her *again*.

We never should have gotten married. I had always known she had ambitions bigger than what she could achieve in Sweetbriar, but I had convinced myself I could love her enough to make her happy. And like the stupid, lovesick fool I had always been for her, I'd just done it again.

"So, you're not staying? I thought since you had your own place this time—"

"Cade, let me explain—"

"You know what? Let's not bother." My heart constricted painfully. I pressed a hand to it and stood. "Obviously, this was a mistake. Sweetbriar will never have what you need."

I will never have what you need . . .

Her feet hit the floor, she stood and tried to catch my eye. "No, that's not it at all—" Her gorgeous blue eyes glittered like she was about to cry. I had to look away. Her tears had always bent me to her will. I couldn't never bear to see her cry.

"We should just quit while we're ahead. Don't you think? Dragging up the past, old feelings, memories . . . It's all pointless when you were never planning to stay. Why would you—"

"Please, I didn't mean—"

"You made a fool of me, Charlotte. I can't believe you would do this to me again and I—I fell for it. How could you?"

"I would never. I—it isn't what it seems. Trent and I—"

"Save it, please. I don't want to know about you and Trent. The thought of you loving somebody else, marrying someone else, being in a bed that isn't mine— it all makes me sick to my stomach. I know we're divorced, but I can't help how I feel." I had no claim over her while we were separated, I knew I was wrong, but I couldn't stop the words from coming out of my mouth.

"Okay, but it's not what it looks—"

"I loved you, Charlotte. More than myself. More than the entire world. I would have done anything to make you stay with me. Why wasn't that enough for you?"

"It had nothing to do with you! You knew it then and you damn well know it now," she bit out. "And it isn't true anyway. You *wouldn't* do anything for me. You let me leave without you!" She bent, slipped her boots on, then stood up to head for the door.

"Yeah, that's right, I guess I did. So leave again. Typical."

"Who are you right now, Cade?" Eyes flashing blue fire met mine as she turned back to glare at me.

Her temper burned beneath the surface just as hot as I remembered it, scorching me alive as I stood there like a fool waiting for her to explain herself and desperate for her to make me believe it.

"I'm not the man you used to know, Charlotte. You broke me."

"You broke me too. I had a full scholarship to NYU, my dream school. I told you I wanted to go to college, and you told me we should break up. I loved you too, you know. I put off my dreams and married you, hoping I could make you change your mind and come with me. I didn't have to wait years to resent you for it, Cade. I resented it almost immediately. Staying here was slowly killing me, and you refused to see it. You wouldn't wait for what you wanted so I could have what I needed. All you cared about was yourself. Sweetbriar is still here, you know. You could have gone to college with me! You got accepted too! Then we could have come right back here and started our lives together—"

"I don't want to talk about this anymore." I stepped around her, picked up our plates and headed for the kitchen.

"I'm not trying to fool you or hurt you. Please believe that." Her voice was faint, but I heard her.

I didn't answer. No words would be adequate enough to describe the pain I felt at this moment, and being vulnerable in front of her was the last thing I wanted now.

"I'll leave. I'm sorry." She snatched her purse from the counter behind me.

"Goodbye, Charlotte." I scraped our plates into the sink then opened the dishwasher to load it.

Her footsteps clicking over the wood floor gave me a sense of finality that burned. I was tempted to stop her, to talk it out and understand where she was coming from. Or maybe try to get her to stay this time. Clearly, I was a glutton for punishment.

A shuddering sigh escaped me, and I looked out the window for a distraction. It was dumping snow like crazy out there and judging by what my backyard looked like, it had been doing it for hours.

"Hey, wait!" I ran through the house to catch her, but she was gone. Opening the front door, I stepped outside to the porch. She was in her Jeep but hadn't started it yet. "Charlotte, stop!"

Her hands swept beneath her eyes. *Shit.*

"I'll be fine, Caden," she shouted. "I know how to drive in the snow, remember?"

"Not in that old Jeep. You don't even have snow tires on it. Let me take you home. Please." I'd never forgive myself if something happened to her. "I'm getting my boots. Do not start that Jeep."

She bit her lip and nodded.

I got my things and clicked the garage door open. She

met me inside but refused to meet my eyes. I couldn't blame her. "It's safer this way."

"I know. That Jeep would never make it up the hill on Maple, and I do not want to spend the night freezing my butt off in the street. So, thank you."

"You're welcome." We got in my SUV. I cranked the heater up. "Warm enough?"

"Yeah. It's fine." She didn't look at me. Her gaze was stuck outside the passenger window as I backed out and turned around.

The drive into town was quiet, the warm breeze from the heater and the crunch of my tires over the road the only sounds. It was dark, but the glare my headlights created through the swirling white outside lit up the cab. She was upset. The tilt of her jaw, her hand tucked beneath her chin, and the stiffness in her posture told me she couldn't wait to get away from me and I felt terrible for reacting so poorly before.

I pulled into her driveway. The need to apologize to her burned in my heart. "We're here. Charlotte, I—"

"*I* don't want to talk anymore, okay," she choked out. "Not right now, anyway."

"I understand. I'm—" She turned to glare at me, and I shut my mouth. My apology could wait. Dad always said an apology given to someone who was still hurt and angry could sometimes be seen as self-serving and he was right. I'd hurt her, and she was entitled to her feelings.

"One of my brothers will get my Jeep when the weather clears." She shoved her door open, grabbed her purse and stepped out, shutting the door with a hard slam.

I watched her dig through her purse for her keys as she made her way to her front door. Her walkway was slippery, and she was wearing high heeled boots, terrible for walking in the snow.

"Damn it!" She slipped backward, landing on her ass in a pile of snow. I stepped out of my vehicle to help but she waved me off. "Just leave me alone, Caden. I'll live, okay?" She batted my outstretched hand away and struggled to her feet. She slipped over the slick stone walkway, softly cursing as she shuffled toward her front deck.

"Your landlord should be ashamed of himself. McMillon, right? Why doesn't he hire a service to shovel and apply deicer to the walkway? This is treacherous even for me, and I'm in snow boots. And I know about the garage. Would you like me to talk to him for you?" I took her arm before she pitched forward into the snow. "This is dangerous, Charlotte. If you parked in the garage, you could use the inside door."

"*Hmph.* Yeah, McMillon, he's a real frickin' peach and I can handle him myself, thanks. I'm a grown up. I'll text him in the morning and take care of it, okay?"

I didn't answer. I knew this attitude. She was upset and trying not to cry by covering it with anger. I had always found it endearing and sweet, and it made me want to protect her.

My own anger had burned out and I felt like an asshole. All I wanted to do now was make her feel okay again.

We made it up the stairs to her front porch, which was even slicker than the path. It was covered by an overhang, so no snow had reached it, but it was dotted with patches of moss and soaking wet. We skidded across the wood together and came to rest up against the door. I held the frame for balance while she unlocked it.

"Don't say a word," she grumbled. "I know. This porch sucks."

Fighting a smile, I looked away, but my eyes caught on a glimmer hanging around her neck. All traces of amusement disappeared when I recognized what it was.

"You're wearing my ring around your neck, Charlotte. Did you explain to your husband what it was? Or did you take it off before you took him to bed with you?"

Chapter 10
Charlotte

"I never took it off." I glared at him as he reached out, touching the gold band dangling between my breasts with a fingertip. It slipped over his index finger and he smiled faintly but there was no light in his eyes, only hurt.

"You kept a piece of me with you," he whispered, letting that trace of a smile drift away as his eyes darted from mine.

"Like I said, I never took it off. I like it where it is." My voice shook. The anger that had kept me going during the drive home had blended with nostalgia and doubt, leaving me vulnerable. I didn't want to feel this way. I wanted to go inside and hide from the pain in his eyes.

His chest heaved. He was angry again, but I was too. This entire situation pissed me off. I added stubborn and demanding and bossy to the list of his qualities that I had forgotten about over the years.

I slipped my fingers between the buttons of his Henley, popped them open, and tugged it down. "What did you tell your girlfriends about this?" I let my other hand slap against his tattoo—*my tattoo*. My name, in script, right over his heart.

His jaw ticked in frustration. "I didn't have to tell them anything. I stayed in Sweetbriar, remember? Everyone in town knows what it did to me when you left."

"Don't be a jerk. Everyone also knows it was way more complicated than that."

He stepped back and the chain broke, the ring still caught on his finger.

"Give me back my ring." I reached out to swipe it, but he held it away from me.

"I bought it. I gave it to you. I was the one who put it on your finger. Maybe I should keep it."

"Give it to me, Cade."

He stuffed the chain in his pocket then pressed the ring against my lips, using it to draw it a line down my chin and neck and stopping between my breasts. "Tell me what you told him Charlotte. He had to see it, hanging right here. Were there others?"

"No. It wasn't like that, we—"

"Shh. I changed my mind." His head shook side to side as his eyes bored into mine. "I don't want to know. It's none of my business what you did while we were apart." He drew the ring back up, pressing it against my lips again and bowing forward until his mouth was inches from mine. "Tell me to leave you alone." The pained growl in his voice made me shiver.

"No. I won't tell you that." My breath caught in my throat. Leaving me alone was the last thing I wanted him to do.

He moved in closer, pressing a hard kiss to my mouth before burying his face in my neck and wrapping me up in his arms. "Tell me to stop." His words were a deep groan against my skin.

"I don't want you to stop." I gripped his jacket at the collar, holding on so he couldn't move away from me.

"Charli baby, are we doing this?" He nipped my neck with a soft bite. It tickled. "Please, tell me I can stay with you tonight. I would die to be inside you again."

"Oh yeah, we're doing this. I want you, Cade. I've never stopped wanting you, and the most important thing I've learned through all these years apart is to take what I want when I can get it. We can figure the rest out later, complications be damned."

He stood straight and brushed the hair from my face. "I've missed you, Charlotte. More than I knew, more than I was willing to admit."

"Come inside, Cade." I tugged him in, kicking the door shut and locking it behind us. "Take off your clothes," I demanded as I let my purse fall to my feet, threw my coat and scarf to the floor, and toed my boots off.

His jacket joined mine, then the Henley and his boots. "Hurry," he demanded. But I froze instead, caught up in watching his forearms flex as he unbuckled his belt, slid it out of the loops, and undid the top button of his jeans.

With a dark smile, he stepped close to me and seized my face between his palms, kissing me rough and thorough. His tongue demanded entrance, which I happily gave him as he walked me backward to the staircase. "Get these off." Warm hands traveled to my waist, and slid into my panties, lowering them along with my pants.

With a wiggle, I stepped backward up the stairs and out of my pants. "My bedroom is up here," I murmured. I turned around and held my hand behind my back to reach for his. Cool air hit my bared lower half and I shivered with anticipation.

I only made it a few steps up before he turned me to face him with his hands at my hips and kissed me breathless. "I can't wait that long. I need you right now."

"God, yes." I sat and he knelt between my legs on the step below me.

I splayed my hands over his bare chest, fascinated by the changes in him, by the hard planes and angles of his body, the ripple of his abs, the strength in his arms . . .

With a reach down, I tugged at his jeans and underwear then watched as he stood to finish removing them. "Cade, please," I whimpered as his cock sprang free. I wrapped my hand around his hard length, opening my mouth and leaning in to taste him but he pulled back.

"We have time for that later." A wicked gleam hit his eyes as he knelt again and pressed his middle finger, with my ring resting at the knuckle, against my lips. His other hand lifted my sweater, and I raised my arms so he could slide it over my head and toss it behind him.

I whimpered as his big hand traveled down my body, between my breasts and down, trailing that ring on a path that led straight between my legs. His bent finger stopped on my clit, and I could feel the cool press of the ring resting against it. "Please," I begged him. "I need you too."

"I don't have a condom with me. Do you have one?" I shook my head no. "Okay, I get tested, I'm safe. Are you on birth control?"

I sucked in a sharp breath when he tapped the ring against my clitoris, then stroked me gently with it as he waited for me to answer.

Normally, I would demand a condom. But I trusted Cade. "Yes, I am, and I'm safe too. I want you, Cade. Right now. Please. I'm saying yes."

Not even a second later and he was inside of me. We both gasped when our hips met and he was fully seated, stretching me open with the wide girth of his cock.

No one else had ever made me feel like this, not ever. With Cade, I was always ready for it. He gripped my hands above my head and pumped into me, giving us both what we had been missing for way too long.

My head lolled back on my neck, touching the stair above and he bent down, tracing his tongue in the hollow of my throat as he interlocked our fingers and I held on tight.

"I remember this. You're perfect, Charli. So fucking

gorgeous. Soft and wet and slick, like heaven wrapped up in hot silk." His words, growled against my skin, drove me insane.

It was out of body, other-worldly, like nothing I would ever have again except with him. Only with him.

My toes curled as he bent and licked his way to a nipple, sucking it into his mouth with one hard pull. I could come like this, and he knew it; he remembered. He sucked harder and I moaned against the top of his head as he released one of my hands to pinch the other nipple between his thumb and forefinger, rolling it firmly and twisting it exactly how I liked.

"Cade, oh god, you remember . . ."

"How could I ever forget anything about you?" he grunted.

He moved harder inside me, faster. My bare skin against the edge of the stair burned but I didn't care, I was about to explode into a million little pieces.

He raised his head and braced his hands on the step above me. His eyes blazed into mine with intent and I nodded, lifting my knees, so my feet rested near my hips as he took me, spreading myself wide, taking every hard inch he gave as he thrust wildly into me.

I clutched his shoulders for balance. Our foreheads pressed together, and our eyes locked as we spiraled out of control, losing ourselves in each other like we had done time and time again back when we were married. Every muscle in my body tensed in a wave, my clit pulsed, and my skin tingled. I could feel him growing impossibly harder as he surged inside then ground himself into me, like he couldn't get deep enough, like he wanted to crawl inside my skin and stay there forever.

"Just like this, Cade, don't stop." He moved in and out with that same brutal press against my clit at the end until I was gasping his name and begging him to make me come.

"Fuck, Charlotte. You feel so good. So fucking good. No one has ever made me feel like you do. No one. Only you."

He reached between our bodies to pinch my clit, then pressed his thumb against it to slide it in circles as he pounded rapidly into me. That was all it took to send us both over the edge. We stayed like this for a minute; him buried deep, cock still pulsing as we caught our breath, panting against each other's mouths as we came down. He kissed me quickly, then brushed my hair back with his eyes smiling into mine.

"Damn, Charlotte." He gasped as his chest heaved from exertion. "Let me take you to bed." We both gasped as he slipped out of me, then stood to pick me up and carry my limp body up the stairs, which I appreciated because I had definitely lost the power to walk. My legs were jelly.

We reached my room where he set me down gently and kissed my forehead. I stepped into the bathroom to clean up. I found him lying in my bed when I came out and immediately went to join him, snuggling into his side as he flipped the covers over us. "Let's go to sleep, Charli. We'll talk tomorrow. Okay?"

"Yeah, Cade. Suddenly, I'm exhausted."

"Same. Night, baby," he whispered as he pulled me tighter.

Despite not knowing where we stood and having not resolved anything with him—other than the fact that we could still fuck each other into a mindless oblivion—I fell asleep easily. He felt like warmth and familiarity, like safety and home, a fact that disconcerted me seeing as how by this point, we'd been apart in this life more than we'd been together.

* * *

I woke up alone.

The storm from last night was nothing but a memory. The sunlight through my window belied my mood, casting me in a light I could not feel. I blinked against the glare and sat up, grabbing the robe at the foot of my bed to cover my nudity.

Where did he go?

I got up, shivering against the chill in the air. Despite the sun, it was still cold, and I hadn't turned the heat up last night. I descended the stairs and headed to the kitchen. The aroma of coffee greeted me, and there was a note near my coffee maker with my ring sitting on top of it.

"Work early. Talk soon."

Cade could be succinct, but that was ridiculous. The writing didn't even look like his either. Did handwriting change over time? *Gah! This sucks!*

I poured a cup, trying to keep my feelings under

control. After the night we'd just spent together, that was all he had to say to me? He hadn't even woken me up to say goodbye.

I shuffled into my living room to sit by the window. I sipped my coffee as everything we did came back to me in a wave of both mental images and bursts of physical memory. I was sore in places that had not been been touched in a long time—my nipples still tingled from his fingers and mouth, I was tender between my legs, and my thighs burned like I had run ten miles last night.

My cheeks heated as I recalled the words he'd whispered in my ear and how he had remembered everything that would turn me on the most. He could still drive me out of my head, make me let go of everything and just feel. We'd made love as if we had been transported to the past, as if our bodies had known nothing of the pain we had caused each other when we separated.

When we were still married, we'd often gotten caught up in each other's bodies rather than working through our differences with words. But to be fair, we only had one real problem, and that was time. I needed time to go to college and chase my dreams and he didn't want to give it to me. Waiting for what he wanted was not Cade's strong suit.

I watched the glittering snow fall out of the trees as it melted. I knew he didn't trust me. The hurt left over from when I left Sweetbriar still lived inside of him. Maybe it would never go away. Could I be with someone who didn't believe in me?

Regret burned through me. It had been way too soon

to get physical with him. My confused feelings were now tangled up so much I worried I would never be able to sort them out.

Chapter 11
Cade

"I'm just saying, maybe you shouldn't have had sex with her yet." Rose plunked a plate in front of me. The scent of bacon and eggs wafted into my nostrils, making my mouth water. "Getting physical too early in a relationship will make you both get twitchy and insecure. Like, your bodies are all in, ready to fall in love, but your brains are still stupid with doubt. Ask me how I know."

"I don't want to know how you know. Please don't tell me. And who says we had sex? Don't make assumptions." I folded a piece of bacon into my mouth and dodged my know-it-all sister's eyes.

Her left eyebrow tipped up as she filled our mugs with coffee then sat down in the chair across from mine at her kitchen table. "Yeah, because you always show up at my house at six in the morning smelling like Charlotte's perfume. Give me a freaking break, Cade."

Trevor kissed the top of her head as he entered the

kitchen then stole her mug, sipping it as he crossed to the stove to fill a plate for himself. "Don't bother arguing with her. It will be fruitless," he remarked.

"Fine, okay, I agree it was too soon but we—sorry, but I can't talk about this topic with you here, Rose."

"I get it. I know it's weird for you now. Trevor and I are married, you two are partners. Whose secrets get kept? Whose get spilled? Who even knows?" She shrugged and stuck her tongue out at me.

"Let's not forget the fact that you live in Gram's house," I added. "Which is pretty weird. I can't imagine being in her old room with a woman. I don't know how you two do it." Trevor had rented our grandmother's house when he moved to Sweetbriar and now that they were married, they were in the process of buying it from her.

"It's not weird for me because I have no memories associated with this place—and just saying, we do it the normal way," Trevor quipped. "Most of the time, anyway." He winked at Rose over his shoulder, and she turned bright red. I was glad she was happy, but this was the very definition of too much information. I was beginning to regret stopping by.

I chuckled in response and shook my head.

"Okay, okay, no more sex talk," Rose insisted. "Can we talk about something else? Anything else, please."

"Fine by me," I agreed. "We don't need to know these things about each other. It's not natural."

Trevor sat next to Rose, and she stole her mug back

with a grin. "Is everything else with her going okay?" he asked me.

"Not really. She isn't staying in Sweetbriar. I guess I was stupid to assume she was—"

"What?" Rose was surprised. "I thought she was staying too. She rented a townhouse this time. Mom said she goes to Vi's shop for coffee almost every day, and she's been getting reacquainted with all of us. I mean, we're supposed to have lunch together next week, I have her number, she's back in Mom's girl's group text—"

"I didn't even have her number. I had to get it from Violet." I raked a hand through my hair in frustration. Damn, it really was a mess. I should have gone home or stayed and waited for Charlotte to wake up. The feeling that I had royally messed things up by leaving was starting to weigh on me.

"Give it a day or two to let the hormones die down, then talk to her about it," Trevor suggested. "Tell her how you feel. Maybe it will change her mind and she'll stay."

"That's what I was thinking too. I left a note on her counter explaining how I feel and that we should talk later after we both settle down. It's a long note. Maybe too long? I filled up a whole page. Shit, now that I think about it maybe I should go get it back before she wakes up?"

Trevor was sympathetic. "No, leave the note. You should always be honest with your feelings. Don't learn about that the hard way."

"Yeah, plus, it's no use trying to talk about anything

serious when neither of you can keep it in your pants," Rose added.

"I thought we were changing the subject." I laughed. "And I don't get why you're assuming we slept together. I haven't actually said a word about it."

Rose rolled her eyes at me. "Dude, go look at your hair in the mirror. And check out your neck while you're there. You're a walking hickey fest and she clearly still wears the same perfume she always did because you smell so much like her she might as well be sitting here instead of you. It's just like being back in high school all over again. Remember when you used to sneak in the hallway window after curfew? Flashback!"

I cleared my throat. "Oh. God." I had come straight here. I guess I should have gone home first. "I didn't know you knew about that."

"Are you serious? We knew everything. Well, not Mom and Dad. They had no clue. But the rest of us did. Why do you think you never got caught? We covered for your loud ass all the time, jeez. It's a miracle you became a cop because you were *so* not stealthy back then. And next time you're trying to keep your nightly activities a secret, shower before you go out visiting people. Or buy some more of that cheap ass body spray you used to hose yourself down with." Her laughter made me smile despite my embarrassment.

"Give him a break, princess," Trevor chided teasingly. "He only has one hickey, and this is a huge deal for the two of them."

"Yeah, *princess*." I smirked. "This is a big deal. And you need at least three hickeys in order to have a fest."

Rose rolled her eyes. "Don't ruin my pet name, Cade. I worked hard to earn that."

"Yeah, you did." Trevor planted a kiss on her lips then grabbed their apparently shared mug of coffee and took a sip, winking at her over the rim. "The kids are still asleep, Rosalie."

"Uh, I have to go." My chair scraped back as I stood up to leave. I knew how to take a hint. "Thanks for breakfast."

"Bye, Cade. We'll talk later." This was Trevor's day off. I should have known better than to stop by.

"Later." I booked it to the door, turning the lock on the knob before letting myself out.

I stopped in the driveway when I heard my name called.

"Hey, Cade." Gwen had moved into the house next door a few months back. She was on her porch, a steaming cup of coffee in her hand.

I wasn't surprised to see her; I knew she was an early bird and got up at the crack of dawn to enjoy some alone time before she woke her kids and started her day. The fact that she was sitting on the lap of Charlotte's brother, Brody's? Now, that was a huge surprise. I wondered if Charlotte knew about them.

"Cade," he greeted and waved me over.

"Hello, you two." I had to school my surprised expression. *Should I ask what was going on? Was it even my business?*

"No, Charlotte doesn't know." Brody informed me with a smirk once I reached the porch.

"Not yet, but she will soon." Gwen confirmed. "How are things?"

"Fine . . ." I hedged. "Hey, can I borrow your snow shovel? I want to clear the front of her place before I go home. Charlotte said she was going to text old man McMillon to do it, but I doubt it will do any good."

"He's a cheap ass, for sure. Go for it – the shovel is propped against the side of the house. You've always been such a sweetheart, Cade."

"Ha, thanks."

"Look, Brody and I aren't a secret, so you don't have to keep it from her. We're going to tell her whenever we can all be in the same place at the same time. We've barely had a chance to catch up since she's been back." She gestured behind herself toward the house. "Kids, work—you know how it is."

"I get it. I doubt it will come up anyway. I'll bring the shovel back on my way home." It wouldn't come up because I was going to do what Trevor said and wait a day or two, which was what I had intended anyway. I needed time to get my head straight so we could talk and not let past hurts get in the way of the future I hoped we could rebuild together. I really messed up with her last night when I saw Trent on the news.

"Later, man." I waved at Brody as I headed to the side of the garage for the shovel then took off for Charlotte's.

I pulled up in front of her townhouse. "Huh." Her place was cleared of snow, the driveway, up the path, and including the porch steps. She must have sent old McMillon a text after all. Good for her. All she needed was for him to clear out the garage. Then she wouldn't have to worry about slipping and sliding her way up to the front door.

I dropped the shovel back at Gwen's and headed home with Charlotte on my mind.

My house was quiet, still, lonely. Precisely as I had left it last night.

Back when Charlotte lived here, I never knew what to expect when I got home. Would she be burning dinner in the kitchen? Waiting for me in the doorway, naked and ready to jump my bones? Or so deep into her writing she barely noticed when I arrived? It never bothered me when she was wrapped up in her stories. I found it inspiring. I loved taking care of her, and she always gave as good as she got.

Our marriage was short lived, but I was beginning to think it had been the best years of my life.

Fuck, I missed her.

Losing her had set me up for over a decade's worth of heartbreak. Not only did I lose her, but I had also lost every possibility I would ever have to find love, because she was it for me.

Last night proved it.

For the first time in years, I felt alive again.

How had I failed to see I had been living in the dark all this time without her? I should have fought harder for her.

And how would I come to terms with the fact that the

best years of my life were the exact same years she regretted?

Chapter 12
Charlotte

I should be working, but instead I called Trent. It was three hours later in New York. Everybody I knew in Sweetbriar would be asleep. Well, except for Cade and I didn't want to call him for obvious reasons. Plus, an update on the stalker situation beyond our daily text check in would be good. So far, he was working, strolling through all the New York tourist places, enjoying Big Mac lunches, and going straight home. Stalking me must have been his only hobby. He had been quiet since I left New York.

"Yeah, Trent. I'm fine. I'm not saying there aren't any nut jobs in Sweetbriar, there's plenty. It's just that anyone local knows not to screw with me. My brothers will put the hurt on anyone who messes with me and I'm on a first name basis with almost all the cops in town. My ex-father-in-law is the police chief for goodness' sake. And of course, you know all about Cade."

Trent wanted to come to Sweetbriar. He was concerned that my asshole stalker would somehow give him the slip and get to me before he could send out a warning. It was silly, but I always tried to avoid saying or even thinking his actual name as if acknowledging it somehow gave him a power over me. He also wanted me to tell my family and the police here in Sweetbriar about him, but I refused. No way. I liked my freedom too much.

"Okay, then I'll stay here in New York and keep following Creepy McStalkerpants around. I can't believe I'm doing this. I'm not a professional and I'm stretched kind of thin since I'm still in play rehearsals. I don't want to miss anything and put you at risk. At least let me hire a hit man or maybe a sexy private detective I can have a fling with—I have money now and I don't mind. Or I could always just kick his ass myself."

"Murder isn't always the answer, Trent," I teased. "But I guess I wouldn't mind if you gave Weirdo VonStalkerton a beat down. Maybe it would scare him off for good."

"Don't make me laugh! Look at what you write! Murder, mayhem, and dead bodies piled up all over the pages. Uh-huh, sure. Violence is your bread and butter, Charli. And look, I'm just waiting for that motherfucker to step a toe out of line. I may joke around with you, but I take your safety seriously. You're my best friend. I love you."

"I love you too. I know you worry about me. And I appreciate it, Trent. You rock as an ex-husband."

"And you're the best ex-wife ever. The next person I

marry will probably be pissed at the pre-nup they'll have to sign now that I finally got the fifty mil. Stay safe. I'll check in tomorrow. Bye Charli."

"Bye." I set the phone down.

I was showered, dressed, and caffeinated. My laptop was open, my manuscript ready and waiting. I should be writing but all I could think about was banging Cade on the stairs again. Or maybe banging him in my bed, or on this couch, or the floor. Damn, I wanted him, and I couldn't find it in myself to care about anything else. My writing mojo was deader than the latest victim in my manuscript, who had just died of an overdose of rat poison disguised as a tragic woodchipper accident—obviously, I had some residual feelings of anger from last night to work through.

I flopped back against the cushions, throwing an arm over my forehead in the most dramatic fashion I could muster.

This sucked.

His curt note still stung a bit, but I managed to rationalize it away for the moment and not burst into tears because he had to be feeling just as weird as I was about our sexy staircase escapade last night.

"*Ughhhh.* Screw this." I had to get out of here before I went stir crazy.

Cade had told me he didn't mind if I worked at Violet's. I shot a text to Dahlia to see if she could meet me. Naturally, she was already there and told me to come on down.

I was feeling better already. I'd get some writing

done, and if Cade's mother happened to drop a few nuggets of information about how he was feeling about me, it would be a happy bonus.

I dug through the bottom shelf of my coffee table for my laptop case and extra charger cord.

"Damn it."

Whatever.

It was obvious I needed a good night of sleep and perhaps a spa trip to clear my head. I was losing everything lately, including my mind. And now that Cade and I had taken it to the next level, I was losing my heart too. I darted upstairs to my room and grabbed a backpack. I stuffed my wallet, laptop, and other necessities in and headed outside to get the heck out of dodge.

Shoot! My Jeep was still at Cade's. I threw my hands up, frustrated. "Double damn." Violet's coffee shop was close. It was cold as heck, but the sun was out. "Screw it." I shoved my keys in my pocket and took off walking.

Sweetbriar in spring could often be described as winter part two, and today was no exception. I was only halfway down the block, and I was already freezing my ass off. "Jeez, this fricking sucks. Literally the worst day ever." I continued ranting to myself as I walked with my breath puffing out in little clouds as I crunched over the—thankfully shoveled—sidewalk. I was going to drink the crap out a hot and steamy huge-ass vanilla latte, and decided maybe I'd get a chocolate croissant too. My standard blueberry muffin didn't feel like enough of a reward for living through this shitty morning. Blueberries were delicious but felt too healthy for my mood.

Finally, I made it to the little strip mall where Vi's shop was located. It was adorable and mountain-y—New York had nothing like this. The long building was built to emulate the look of a log cabin, with dark wood and stacked stones, big beams, and forest green trim. Little planters were filled with evergreen shrubbery and tiny topiaries glittered with clear lights wrapped around their trunks.

This town was charming as hell. When the weather grew warm, each light pole would hold a hanging basket overflowing with flowers from the local nurseries and the empty lot at the end of the street would be filled with little stands for area farmers to sell their produce.

With each step I grew angrier with myself. Why had I stayed away for so long? I loved it here. This was my home, not New York.

By the time I got inside Violet's I was grumpy, and a little bit pissed off. I did this sometimes—got myself worked up over something that was my own fault.

"Hey, Charlotte!" Violet called. "The usual?"

"Not this time. A vanilla latte, extra hot, and something chocolate please."

"Oh crap, girl, you're ordering something different. What did my bonehead brother do to you?"

Startled laughter burst out of me. "How did you know? I mean, he didn't do anything really—"

"One, your face always tells the tale. You've always been a wide-open book. And two, duh, he's my brother and I love him to pieces, but I know for a fact that he can also be a stubborn horse's ass sometimes. He needs to learn how to communicate."

"Well, he left me a note earlier and it was brusque to say the least. I mean, we—um, last night—never mind. I just expected more, I guess. He really didn't do anything. It's my fault for having expectations before we were able to hash everything out."

"I'm so sorry. He'll make it better. Don't give up yet. His heart is good. You know that, right?"

"Yes, I do. His heart is amazing and wonderful, and I missed it so much—uh, which is probably why I'm so grouchy and hurt this morning, I guess." My cheeks burned; I didn't have to spell it out for her to guess what had happened between me and Cade. Her knowing eyes on mine understood everything I hadn't said.

"He disappointed you this morning, didn't he sweet-heart?" Her eyes shined with sympathy. From the little I'd heard around town about her situation with her ex-husband, she definitely understood disappointment.

I nodded rather than answer with words. Tears burned behind my eyelids and I blinked furiously to clear them. I didn't want to cry in front of Violet and push her sweet sympathy too far, especially considering how I was the one who had broken her brother's heart all those years ago.

"Go on and sit with Mom. I'll bring your order to you. Take a load off."

The idea of working with Dahlia excited me and perked me up a bit. Getting to be with her again was one of the reasons I wanted so badly to stay in town. "I'm here to work with your mom today. I'm going to soak up all her writerly vibes and get loaded up on coffee and carbs and forget all about what happened last—"

"Oooh la la. I won't ask. I'll just make all kinds of assumptions."

I laughed. "Go right ahead. I don't kiss and tell. For the most part, anyway."

"I'll be there in a minute."

"Thank you, Vi. I—I missed you when I was gone. I want you to know that."

"Oh, Charli, I know, and I missed you too." She had been the best sister-in-law, so sweet. We'd have lunch once a week and discuss books and life. We were both big readers, and I had helped her set up her book club. We used to have such fun together.

Choked up again, I nodded, then turned to head to Dahlia's usual table in the corner. Cade's dad was there too. Ben Barrett was one of the best men I knew. He was honest and kind and had always been like a second father to me.

"Hey, honey, come on over." His enthusiastic wave threatened to spill the tears I'd been holding back. I inhaled a sharp breath to steady myself and waved back.

"Hi, you two. Dahlia, thank you for letting me crash your writing session."

"Any time, sweetheart. Maybe we can sprint if we get our motivation up. But I'm having a lazy day so far, so no guarantees."

Sprinting consisted of setting a timer and writing nonstop until it went off. Sprinting alone sucked, but sprinting with Dahlia would probably be intimidating as hell. The woman had written almost a hundred books.

"That's okay. I love you, but sprinting with you sounds terrifying," I joked. Ben laughed as I set my things down, then slid into the seat next to her at the round table.

She winked at me through her black cat eyeglasses and swept her long silvery blonde hair over her shoulder. "Nonsense. I've read your books. You're wonderful, Charlotte. Don't ever underestimate or underrate yourself. You're gifted. Own it. And side note, Adaline Paige is my current obsession."

Ben chuckled. "Especially since you introduced that small town cop, Officer Jaden Skeritt into the storyline. A little bit of art imitating life, am I right?"

I turned bright red. I hadn't realized I had named him after Cade until the book had been published and it was too late to do anything about it. "God. I am mortified. That was an accident of epic subliminal and deeply Freudian proportions."

"No, I love it. It's a sign about your future with Caden is what it is," Dahlia insisted, pointing her scone at me for emphasis. "You belong with my son. You are part of this family, honey, a Barrett for life. But I promised to keep my nose out of this situation and that's what I'm going to do."

I giggled nervously. Dahlia was known for matchmaking, always getting her way, and ending up correct about almost everything she had ever predicted. She thought Cade and I belonged together. The odds were in her favor, and I supposed mine too since I wanted him back. Or at least I thought I did. The problem was, would I be able to keep him this time? Losing him again would kill me.

"I've got to get back to the station. Cade and Trevor are both off today, and they need a senior officer there." After kissing Dahlia goodbye, he stood and placed a kiss to the top of my head. "I wish you would stick around this time, Charli. Dahlia is right. You're a Barrett for life. Bye now."

"Bye." I breathed. I watched him leave without focusing. My blood had turned to ice, and I was sure my face had turned red again because it was on fire. Even my body was confused. Hot and cold, exactly like my relationship with Cade seemed to be.

Cade was off work today?

He was off.

He was fucking off.

That note: *"Work early. Talk soon."*

Why would he lie to me? Obviously, he couldn't get away from me fast enough. Obviously, he regretted spending the night with me. So, obviously, this would never work between the two of us.

Violet showed up with my coffee and a chocolate filled croissant.

"Thank you." The sound of my voice echoing in my ears was muted, like it had come from under water. I couldn't stay here, but if I left, they would know something was wrong and I didn't want anyone knowing anything about how I felt.

I sipped the hot coffee. I took a bite of my breakfast.

I could do this. I was strong on my own and had been for years.

I had been friends with Dahlia even after the divorce and I didn't want to lose her. "Let's sprint." The good thing about sprinting was there would be no need for talking while we did it.

"You got it, sweetie." She set the timer on her phone, and off we went.

I resisted the urge to kill off Jaden Skeritt in a tragic, yet heinously brutal murder. Blood and guts were totally my bread and butter. Trent had been right about that.

Stabbing was too good for liars.

I was picturing razor sharp guillotines and psychopathic maniacs running amok wielding chainsaws, or maybe an assortment of rusty medieval weapons could accidently be distributed throughout a maximum-security prison that Jaden was somehow trapped inside of . . .

I was also fighting the temptation to write in a sexy lumberjack or burly firefighter for Adaline to mess around with to make Jaden jealous.

But sadly, my heart was a faithful fool even if my imagination always ran out of control. So, instead of imaginary revenge plots, I ended up writing a scorching hot love scene involving Jaden going down on Adaline for hours and hours (and hours. She was angry and incredibly horny, obviously), followed by an epic sexcapade on her staircase, after which he declared his undying love to her. I ended the chapter with a hot air balloon proposal over Mt. Hood.

Adaline was thrilled with her sparkly diamond engagement ring.

Damn it.

Chapter 13
Cade

Waiting to talk to Charlotte was a stupid idea. The regret piled higher after each day had passed. And now I was here at Holloway's, almost a week later, halfway to drunk, and losing my mind over her.

After my third beer, I started thinking seriously about just walking to her townhouse and telling her what was gonna happen between the two of us. Her complex was right across the street; I could see it out the window. Her light was on in the garage, damn it, so she had to be up. I could be over there right now, maybe convincing her to forgive me. Then perhaps we could have another round on the staircase.

She was mine; that's all there was to it. I had to make her understand how I felt. I had to make her see how good we were together and convince her to stay this time.

"I think I'm going to go over there," I said to the table full of my brothers, plus my brothers-in-law, Trevor, Jake, and Luke, and Luke's Army buddy, Liam, who my mother had practically adopted and within months had become like another brother to all of us.

"No, you are not, no fucking way," Asher, the oldest of all us Barrett siblings, declared, laying a hand on my arm when I tried to stand up. His hair was bright red, just like my little sisters, Lily and Rose. The rest of us were boring with various shades of brown.

"You're well on your way to being drunk, you idiot," Jude added. "You'll only end up pissing her off."

Levi just shook his head and sipped his beer, his semi-permanent smirk firmly in place.

"Never talk to your woman when you're drunk and upset," Asher instructed. "You'll end up saying or doing things you will not remember in the morning. Nothing good ever comes from it."

"He's right," Levi agreed. "Happened to me with Becca." Every eye at the table snapped to him. He never *ever* talked about what went down with his childhood sweetheart. In fact, none of us knew what had happened to end their relationship. One day it was just over, and neither one of them said a word about it. He hadn't had that much to drink, but maybe he was just drunk enough to finally spill his guts.

"So, uh, what happened, man?" prodded Jude, his fraternal twin, and the one with the best chance to get him to talk. His tone was as casual as he could make it, even though we were all dying for the story.

"I proposed to her, drunk off my ass. Ring and every-thing, then forgot about it the next morning. She woke up happy and I woke up clueless. And then it was over. To be fair, that wasn't our only problem, it's just the one that sent all the other ones spinning out of control. She'll never forgive me. Hell, she won't even talk to me."

"Dude," I breathed. "That's—I don't even know what to say about it. That's how much it sucks. I'm sorry."

He scratched his dark stubble and shrugged. "It is what it is. I'm going to order some shots. I don't want to be mentally present until at least noon tomorrow." He slid back his chair, then stalked to the bar.

"He saw her at the station today visiting her brother," Jude informed us when Levi was out of earshot. "It was bad."

Luke poked me in the side. "Cade, she's here. Do not look behind you." Of course, I immediately turned and looked. Honestly, everyone should know by now not to tell me that.

Charlotte was hot as hell in a snug black sweater dress and the same high-heeled boots from our night together. She was accompanied by Gwen and my cousin Savannah; they were on their way to a table. She slowed down when she saw me. Her smile was faint as she waved to me, but it didn't reach her eyes. Something wasn't right.

"Charli?" Liam's jaw dropped. "Is that you?" I spun around, watching as he stood up with a huge smile on his face.

"Liam! Oh my god! I haven't talked to you since— well you skipped out on the graduation ceremony, and then we heard you enlisted . . ." Her face was lit up like a

Christmas tree as she ran into his outstretched arms. "You didn't say goodbye to us, you big jerk." She pulled back and lightly slapped him on the arm. "How the hell are you? What are you doing in Sweetbriar? Oh my god, you guys, it's freaking Liam!"

"What's up, freaking Liam?" Luke joked. "We're all waiting. Carry on with the explanation."

Liam chuckled then turned to me. "I had no idea your Charlotte was *my* Charlotte. I can't believe I didn't put it together."

I froze. *His Charlotte?*

Did they?

Had they?

What the fuck was going on?

I had to remind myself I had no right to be angry, no matter what had gone on between them. "Your Charlotte?" I questioned through my clenched jaw.

Liam's eyes went soft with sympathy while Charlotte continued deliberately avoiding my eyes. "Hey, no worries, Cade. Not that kind of mine, okay? We went to NYU together. We were both in the writing program." He turned back to Charlotte "Hey, how's Trent doing?"

"He's great." Her smile came back at the mention of her ex-husband, and I scowled. I was barely hanging on. I felt like punching someone, but unfortunately, there was no one around who deserved it. "His play just opened. He's on Broadway, Liam!"

"Damn, that's amazing! Just what he always wanted."

"Yeah, so he's doing great."

Liam's eyes shifted between me and Charlotte. I

could see his mind working as he put the pieces together. He obviously knew everything. "And you?" He asked her softly as he eyed me. "How are you doing, Charli?"

"Fine, of course. Uh, I'm doing great—"

"Are you still writing?"

An embarrassed puff of air escaped her, blowing back a wayward curl. "You could say that . . ."

"Ever heard of Keli Marlowe?" Gwen asked Liam as she nudged Charlotte's shoulder with hers.

"The murder mystery author? No shit? Oh, Charli, you did it."

Charlotte beamed. "Yeah . . ."

I couldn't take it anymore. "I'm getting another pitcher." I stood. "Anyone want anything while I'm at the bar?" I all but ran off without waiting for an answer.

Jealousy and regret ate at me. There were so many aspects of her life that I hadn't been part of. So much that I didn't know about her—where she'd been, what she'd done. Who she had been with when she should have been with me.

Fuck, I had no right to these feelings. I was the one who had screwed things up for us. I had been impatient, unyielding, stubborn. I let her go when I should have made a compromise. I should have done whatever it took to keep her in my life.

I had been a fool, and now I was paying for it.

"Cade. Rough night?" My cousin Oliver was out of the kitchen for once and serving drinks behind the bar.

"To say the least," I mumbled. "I came here to blow

off some steam. I have to be able to talk to her without sounding like a possessive dick. But every day that goes by makes it worse. And I'm not sure how to handle myself."

He filled up a glass with ice and a Coke. "No more alcohol. You need your head in the game tonight."

"You got that right." I took the Coke. "Thanks."

"Yup. Food?"

"No thanks. Not tonight."

"Take it easy. And help me keep an eye on this one." His head tilted toward Levi before he moved down the bar to help another customer.

I sat in the stool next to Levi, who was currently not taking Oliver's "no more alcohol" advice. Several empty shot glasses were lined up in front of his seat at the bar. His eyes were red-rimmed and sad.

"You okay?"

"Fuck no." He downed another shot then slammed the glass next to the others. "This is my last one though. I'm not an idiot. I'm exactly drunk enough to forget for the night, but not so drunk I'll end up texting her."

"That's good. Want to talk about it?"

"Nope. I already said too much. Do *you* want to talk?"

"Fuck no."

He snorted. "I figured. You should go talk to her though. Don't let any more time go by. It's stupid."

"You think?"

"You love her, don't you?"

"I don't—" I stopped talking. A denial would be a lie,

but a confirmation would be too soon. I wasn't ready to admit it to myself.

"Go on. Do it. Talk to her. What can it hurt at this point?"

"Yeah, maybe you're right."

"Of course I am. I learn everything the hard way. It sinks in better. If I learn at all, that is." The last part was mumbled under his breath.

He was like a tragedy, sitting here. I wanted to help him. "Maybe Becca—"

"No. It's not possible. Not a chance in hell."

"Okay. We'll talk about it another time."

His eyes slid to the side and met mine. "No, we won't."

I slapped him on the shoulder and stood. "I'm here for you, Levi. Always."

"I know. Go get your girl."

With a quick look behind me, I saw her press a kiss to Liam's cheek then head for a table followed by Gwen and Savannah.

She was away from Liam but still I hesitated, lingering here at the bar before losing my nerve and heading back to my table instead of to hers.

As I approached, Liam stood up and pulled me to the side, away from the listening ears at the table. "Nothing ever happened between me and Charlotte, Cade," he reiterated. "She was just a great friend, and I was in no place in my life to try for anything more back then. Even if I had wanted to."

I nodded. "Thanks for telling me. After the surprise wore off, I could tell."

"I hesitate to say anything, but I feel like I have to because it's obvious you still have feelings for her. She was my friend and we trusted each other, but as wrong as it feels to betray a confidence from the past, it would be worse if I didn't let you know what you might be dealing with. For her sake. Maybe yours too."

The blood froze in my veins. "What is it?"

"She was pretty broken when we met. Devastated would be a vast understatement."

"Oh. I—" I didn't know what to say. I had been broken up over the divorce too. While it hadn't been ugly, bitterness had hung over my head for years after she left, only to be followed by numbness and a refusal to ever let her cross through my mind.

Had it been the same for her?

"You don't owe me any explanations. That's not why I'm bringing it up. From what I understand it was a question of timing and your ambitions not lining up. You were both young." His shoulders shrugged. "Those things happen. But I think you should know that her decision to leave you was not without consequence for her. She was a mess. Luckily, on her first day in New York, she ran into Trent and me. The dude is a riot, funny as hell. He took her under his wing and forced whatever happiness that remained inside of her to the surface. He did the same thing for me."

"I'm glad she had the two of you to lean on."

"Yeah, not as glad as we were to have her. She's a

great person, Cade. I hope you can make her happy again. I would love to see it."

"Why did you leave then?"

"No good reason. My past caught up to me, I guess. I didn't make the best choices when I was young."

"God, did any of us?"

He chuckled. "Probably not."

"I'm glad we talked. I appreciate this, Liam."

He clapped me on the shoulder as we headed back to our table. "You bet. I hope it helps."

"Any insight into what she might be thinking helps."

Charlotte and I were never the best at communicating, which was something I should endeavor to change if I wanted any chance at a future with her.

Chapter 14
Charlotte

Holloway's was busy tonight. I swear, the entire damn town was packed in here and for once I was glad to be stuck in a crowd. I could sit with my girls and avoid Cade, and no one would think anything of it. Our table was in the corner, I had a glass of my favorite wine, and an entire charcuterie board was sitting in front of me. Being besties with one of the owners had definite perks, including no waiting and getting a guaranteed table.

I had said goodbye to Liam with an exchange of phone numbers and a promise that we would have lunch together and get reacquainted. I still couldn't quite believe he was here. He had been a wonderful friend. Without him and Trent, I never would have made it through my first year of college.

"I can't believe that hottie Liam is your old college buddy." Gwen rolled her eyes and took a sip of her mojito. "Only you, Charlotte."

"What do you mean, 'only me?'" I sipped my wine and slid the charcuterie board closer. This was a going to be a night to remember, for sure. I needed sustenance.

"First of all, hello? Take a look at your brothers. All five of them are hot as hell. Everyone thinks so." I wrinkled my nose. Objectively I could admit they were good-looking, but the word "hot" was not one I would use to describe them because, yuck.

"Especially Brody, right?" I raised my eyebrows and waited for her reaction. I knew about her and Brody. She'd had a crush on him since high school and he had essentially been waiting in the wings for her to ditch her loser ex. It had always been just a matter of availability. As for how I found out? Spencer, brother number five, had a big mouth.

"Uhhhh . . ." She blushed bright red and exchanged a glance with Savannah.

I laughed at both of them. When were people going to realize that nothing got past me? "Okay, let's move along for now. We'll discuss you and Brody another time. By the way, I'm cool with it."

"Thank god! And fair enough. Okay, moving right along." She shook her head. "Damn, Charli. Okay, Trent is literally the sexiest man I've ever seen in my life. You married him and the two of you did not have sex. Like, *how?* And Cade? Just look at him—six-foot-four, ripped to shreds, and those brown eyes?" She fanned herself and waggled her eyebrows at me

"Maybe I get along with dudes because I have so many brothers? I don't know." I shrugged.

She tilted her head as she considered my words. "Maybe. Now let's talk about Liam, shall we? I've seen him around town, and I had no idea you knew him. Who else do you know? Are you buddies with Henry Cavill? Jason Momoa, perhaps? Spill your secrets. I want to build a hot guy harem just like yours."

"Ew." Savannah objected. "I approve of everyone you listed except for Cade. Yeah, he's my cousin and a blood relation, which is an obvious reason. But aside from that, we once spent a family Disneyland weekend stuck in a hotel room together with the stomach flu while everyone else had fun. It was not pretty."

"Gross! And aww, you missed Disneyland!" Gwen laughed and slid the board back to the middle.

"We're gonna need more food, you guys." I eyed the charcuterie board proprietarily. "I'm stressing out."

"You came here to get drunk and unwind, Charli. Order some shots. Get wasted. We're here to take care of you."

"No way, I can't get wasted now. Cade is here. If I'm drunk and he's around, I'll hit on him and that's not fair to cither one of us. Drunk Charlotte is always insatiable for sober Cade. When we were married, I used to give him pre-permission sometimes."

"Pre-permission?" Savannah laughed. "Do I want to know?"

"Pre-permission for sex. He wouldn't have sex with me if I was drunk. I had to, you know, tell him in advance whenever I was in the mood for drunk sex."

Gwen sighed. "See? I knew he was a good guy. That note he left you was an anomaly—"

"No more talking about the note, remember? I've never spent more time thinking about four measly words. I'm done being pathetic. And, yeah, he is the best guy," I agreed. "But seriously, that's a low bar. No one should have sex with a drunk person unless it's preplanned, right? Even if you're together, it could be taking advantage. Cade is a good guy for other reasons." Except for our recent morning-after; that was not good. Leaving me naked in bed with a terse note and my wedding ring on the kitchen counter seriously sucked, even if he had made me coffee.

"They're all good guys," Savannah added. "I mean, Uncle Ben is the best guy ever. After my dad died, he stepped in—father-daughter dances, camping trips, fishing, our various sports games, he was there for all of it. There is no way any son of Ben Barrett could turn out bad. It's not possible. Oh gosh! Shh, don't turn around," she hissed.

Of course, I immediately turned around to see the man himself walking toward our table. "Hey, Cade."

"Charlotte. Can we talk?" His face was unreadable.

"Sure." My mood had turned into a strange combination of mad, sad, wistful, and horny. Basically, I was about to make no sense and confuse the shit out of both of us. Talking to him right now, when I was this unsettled, had *bad idea* written all over it. I swept my eyes across the table. Gwen and Savannah were nodding at me to go with him, but despite their encouraging grins, I didn't feel much hope. I shrugged and stood up. I might as well get this over with.

"Should we go for a walk in the park across the street?" he suggested.

"And freeze our asses off in the dark?" I shrugged. "Sure, why not?" He chuckled as I took his outstretched hand.

After bundling up in our coats, we headed to the park next to my townhouse complex. It was small, but lushly planted with evergreen shrubbery and pine trees. It gave the feel of being deep in the forest. I loved spending time here, but I'd never been here at night.

We reached a stone bench and I sat, grateful it was dry. I looked up at him as he stood there, studying my face, probably trying to find something to say.

"You left early the other day and we haven't talked. I haven't seen you around. Are you okay?" I remarked, my tone deliberately neutral, leaving the conversation open to wherever he decided to take it.

He joined me on the bench and took my hand. "I'm sorry. I shouldn't have done that. I wrote a note. I was feeling overwhelmed—"

"I understand. I was too. The other night was—unexpected."

"You could say that. I didn't plan on what ended up happening. I wanted to get to know you again before we slept together—" He paused. "That isn't what I meant." He leaned forward, elbows to his knees and buried his face in his palms, clearly frustrated. "I mean, I had no expectations of you. I would never expect sex from you, or anyone. Damn it, I didn't invite you to dinner to get you into bed again. Shit, I don't know what I'm saying—"

"Hey, I get you." I ran a hand down his back. "It's okay. We went from having dinner, to arguing, to having sex on my staircase. Kind of like we used to do after a fight, if I recall correctly. Minus the staircase part, which was a happy bonus."

He let out a sad laugh and peeked up at me from the corner of his eye. "We were always good at make-up sex, weren't we?"

"We were always good at all the sex. That was never our problem."

"What was our problem then, Charlotte?" He sat up straight and met my eyes, the vulnerability in his expression busted my heart right open. I almost couldn't take it.

"Youth, I think. We were too young to handle those huge feelings we shared and you know it, Cade. And, timing, obviously. Add in some opposing ambitions, and there you have it."

"Right." He sighed. "That stuff."

"Yup. That stuff . . ."

"But I still want you," he confessed. "I don't know how to feel about that. Ever since you got back, you're all I can think about."

"The feeling is mutual, and confusing as hell. I want you too, Cade."

"We need one more night," he declared.

"What?" I wanted more than one. I had the dreadful feeling that I wanted all his nights, and he would be too afraid I'd leave again to give them to me.

"One more night together to get it out of our system. The other night was an accident. It went by too fast, yet I can't stop thinking about it. I need one more—"

"Are you sure? Like you said, it was an accident. If we spend another night together it will be deliberate. A choice we can't play off as a fluke based on our chemistry. I guess what I'm really saying is I don't want to get hurt. Like, what happens next?"

"But aren't you hurting right now? I am. We have all these feelings built up between us. We were too young when we split to resolve them—"

"And you think spending the night together will bring us some sort of closure?"

"Yeah, I do. At least I hope so."

I had my doubts. I knew I would never be able to get him out of my mind. Spending the night with him would end up being a huge mistake, but I didn't want to say no to him. I wanted to keep the possibility of having him back in my life alive. "Okay. Yes." His eyes flashed and he squeezed my hand. "I'm counting on it now, Cade. You can't take it back," I teased, because I had to lighten the mood.

For now, we were good.

For this moment, I had him back in my life.

Maybe I could just stay in Sweetbriar forever and see what happened. No definitions, no declarations. Just me and him and . . . whatever. We could live *one more night* into infinity.

"I won't take it back. There are things I didn't get to

do to you." His eyes were hot and dark with wicked promise as they burned into mine.

"Oh yeah, like what?" I breathed, pleasantly surprised at the sudden shift in his temperament when I said yes.

"For one, I can't wait to get my mouth between those pretty thighs again. I miss the way you taste." I blinked as a startled thrill shot through me at his words.

"God, Cade. I want that. Do you want me to do that thing you like?"

"I want you to do all the things."

"Will one night be enough? As I remember it, you used to like quite a few of the things I used to do to you."

He grinned and took my other hand. "We'll find out, won't we?"

"My place?" I turned and tugged him along with me as I stood. "Right now? Is your truck at Holloway's? We can move it to my driveway." Instead of following me, he pulled me toward him with a hand at the back of my neck and kissed the hell out of me.

"We really should have just gone straight to my place," I mumbled against his lips, smiling when he chuckled and grabbed my ass.

"You got that right. Let's get out of here. I'll make your favorite breakfast in the morning. I'll even bring it to you in bed and eat you after you eat it."

"French toast! With that whippy vegan cinnamon cream cheese you always stuff in the middle? And maple syrup? Wait, what was that last thing you said?"

He burst out laughing. "Only my sweet Charlotte

would get distracted by the promise of food over the other promise I just made her."

"Oh no, I'm pretty sure I heard you right. You said you'd go down on me after bringing me breakfast in bed. That's, like, every woman's dream. No takesies backsies. It's a done deal." I slid my hands up his hard chest and cupped his cheeks in my palms with a huge smile on my face.

He bit his lip. "God, you're too much. I love it."

I grabbed his hand and spun us around in a circle before finally finding the way out of the park. He laughed as I led him behind me, jogging across the street to the parking lot.

One quick drive across the street and we were in her driveway. I was ready for her. I'd been ready for another night since I walked out of her place after leaving that stupid note.

"Stay here." I ran a hand up her thigh, giving it a gentle squeeze at the top. "I'll come around and open your door. I haven't forgotten about your slippery porch."

"Such a gentleman."

"For now. Once we cross through the front door all bets are off." I wanted to get inside her again. It was literally the only thing I could think about since she said yes.

That was bullshit. I *always* thought of her, even before she said yes to me tonight. Even when I had been with someone else, Charlotte's face was all I could ever see.

My heart was turning somersaults in my chest and the feeling that I would die if I couldn't be with her pounded itself into my head.

Our night together had been pure magic. I'd been riding the high until I realized leaving her naked in bed at the crack of dawn was an asshole rookie mistake and rightly began the process of beating myself up over it. This was my chance to make it up to her. She had to know I'd grown up over the years. That I had changed, and was a better man now.

Quickly, I dashed around to her door. Instead of helping her down and holding her elbow to guide her to the porch, I picked her up and carried her. It was faster, debatably safer, and it definitely felt good to hold her close. Her squeal of surprise didn't hurt either.

"Cade, don't ever stop."

"Stop what?"

"Being sweet. Remembering everything. Taking care of me. Damn it, I've said too much, like usual . . ." Clearly embarrassed by her words, she tucked her head against my chest to hide her face.

"Hey, look at me. I won't stop, okay? I can't. And I love that you feel this way about me. That morning had me rattled. I know I hurt you by leaving and I didn't mean to. I'm so sorry."

"It's okay," she breathed.

I let her slide down my body once we reached her front door. "If you change your mind and just want to talk, it's fine. It would be totally understandable."

"See? Taking care of me. It's kind of irresistible. And I haven't changed my mind." She dug through her purse for her keys then let us inside. "Damn, it's cold in here.

I'm sorry, I thought I turned up the heat before I left. I'm pretty sure I'm losing my mind."

"The deadline for your book stressing you out?"

"Among other things." She tossed her purse to the counter and hung her coat on the hook by the door. "*Ugh*, my neck is killing me."

"I can help with that." I followed suit and hung my coat next to hers. "Turn around."

"Ooh, yes please. Your massages are the best." She spun around and dropped her head forward.

I ran my palms over her shoulders, sliding them up to her neck. "You're not so bad yourself. I remember yours too."

"Why, thank you, kind sir. Turnabout is fair play. But, like, in a nice way. I'll do you next."

I chuckled. "Writing with my mom didn't help?"

"It did. I'm just too far behind. I might have to ask for an extension. I've always been on time, Cade. I hate this."

"It'll be okay, Charli. Just try to relax. One extension out of what? Ten books? That's pretty great as far as I'm concerned."

"Thank you, and you're probably right. Plus, getting worked up over it makes it harder to write. Ohhhh, that feels so good. Let's go up to my room. I need to lie down to fully appreciate this." She pulled away and gestured toward the staircase with a grin.

I held out my arms. "You want a ride up?"

"Heck yes." She hopped up and wrapped her arms and legs around me, relaxing against my chest as I gripped her luscious ass in my hands and carried her up the stairs. "The door on the right."

I opened it and set her down, pulling her close to kiss her with my hands at her hips. "I don't want a massage."

"I just want you to keep your promise." She took my hand and placed it between her legs.

"Trust me, I would die before I broke that promise." I stroked her once, then grabbed the hem of her dress to pull it over her head. "Get those boots off and lie down." She did as I asked while I stripped, threw her covers back and got into her bed.

She joined me. We were face to face on our sides. "Tell me a secret," she murmured. Sometimes we ended our days just like this—whispering our secrets to each other in the dark.

Her hands started in my hair, then cupped my face, before running over my chest, down my abs, to end up wrapped around my cock.

I was in heaven. I couldn't form words, let alone think of a secret to tell her. I was lost in her eyes, lost in the way her hands felt on my body. "I don't think I ever had a crush," I blurted without thinking.

Her eyes softened on mine. "Oh yeah?"

"Yeah. Not a real one, anyway. Fuck, do that again. Harder this time."

She laughed softly and tightened her palms around my cock as she stroked me. "Tell me more, Cade."

"Damn, Charlotte, you're about to undo me and this feels so good I don't even care," I groaned. "It was only ever you, and it was way more than a crush. Even before that Sadie Hawkins dance back in eighth grade. Only you."

Her face lit up and she stroked me harder. "I love that so much."

"I bet you do." I let a hand drift between her bare thighs to slide a finger into her wet heat.

"God, yes, Cade. Show me how much you want me." She shifted her knee up to rest on my hip and I smiled before reaching up to unfasten the silky scrap of a bra she wore and toss it aside.

"Get those panties off. Charli baby, why aren't you naked yet?" I chuckled as I nipped her neck below the ear and stroked her gently, circling her clit then dipping back inside.

"You take them off." Her teasing smile was adorable, but I didn't want to be sweet. It was all I could do not to shove her to her back and devour her.

I moved up to my knees, grabbing the flimsy strings at her waist to tug them down. With a wiggle she lifted her ass so I could slip them down her hips and off. Hands at her knees, I spread her legs apart and rolled to my stomach between them, darting my tongue out to lick and nibble my way up one slim thigh, then down the other, deliberately skipping over the part I was desperate to finally get another taste of.

"Hey, I thought you missed this," she protested with a grin, shifting her hips side to side. She was up on her elbows, watching me.

"Oh, I do, and I'm about to show you exactly how much." I licked up her center in one broad stroke, from that hot, silky opening to her clit.

I was starving for it, ravenous. I licked and sucked and buried my tongue inside her while her feet dug into my shoulder blades and her sexy thighs trapped my head in place.

She tasted as sweet as I remembered her. Honey and spice and all Charlotte. I let out a groan, the sound a deep mixture of agonized pleasure and the desperate urge to fuck her until the only thing she could remember was me and everything we used to share.

But this was all for her, so I gave her my fingers instead, hooking them to find that spot inside that I knew would make her lose her mind while I took that sweet little clit into my mouth, darting my tongue against it and sucking her hard.

Her hands shoved into my hair while soft keening cries fell from her lips. "Cade, don't you dare stop," she mewled as she writhed against my mouth. Her knees drew up, then fell to the sides as she planted her feet on the mattress and thrust her hips against my face.

She was frantic now, hands clawing the sheets, legs straining and spread wide open. I could feel her tightening on my fingers in fluttering waves, so I gave her another one. I moved my tongue faster around her clit, swirled it harder, then sucked it back into my mouth with pulsing little pulls until her legs relaxed, she shuddered against me, and yelled my name.

"I need you now. Get up here, get inside me. *Please*, Cade." She reached for me then, her voice nothing but breathy, shuddering whispers of need as she came down from her high.

I wanted her so much, almost too much. I didn't want this to be over too fast. Slowly, I moved up her body until I could slip inside. She was hot, wet paradise and still trembling from her orgasm.

My eyes slammed shut as I struggled to slow down and be gentle when all I wanted to do was fuck her hard and senseless, until we were both lost in our pleasure and driven out of our minds with lust.

"I love how you feel inside me. Like you belong there." She moaned in my ear. I braced myself over her, moving slowly, easing myself in and out as I watched her eyes drift closed and her lips part as she took me.

"I want to make you feel good." I groaned into her neck, biting gently.

"You do. This is perfect, Cade."

I began to move with deep strokes. Long and slow, smiling as she arched her back and wrapped a leg around my hips, then dug her nails in my back to pull me closer.

I was losing control. She wasn't making it easy to go slow with her sexy panting breaths in my ear, her hands moving down to my ass to pull me in, and the honey sweet taste of her pussy still on my tongue.

She met my thrusts, shoving her hips up into mine, faster and faster until our bodies fell into that same hard rhythm we had always been able to create together.

We were made for each other; we always had been, and it was obvious to me now we always would be.

We were wordless, speaking with moans and sighs, grasping hands, and groans of pleasure.

I went deeper and she bit my earlobe, sucking it into her mouth before she whispered in my ear, telling me not to stop, not to dare fucking stop.

This was full body; every sense was on fire as I burned for her.

Her smell, her taste, the feel of her slick skin enveloping mine was my world. The only thing that mattered was making her explode so I could put her back together again.

She cried out, begging without words for me to make her come. She was mine to please, mine to take care of and protect, and I would do it each and every time she needed me.

Light burst behind my closed lids. My spine tingled as my body tightened for release. She was close too. I could feel it in the way she squeezed me deeper.

I reached the peak, almost ready to let go and fall. I forced my eyes to open. I had to watch her come, I needed to see the flush in her cheeks, the gorgeous arc of her neck, the faint smile that always traced across her face when she came. She was everything beautiful in the world. All I would ever need to be complete, but damn it, she wasn't mine.

And she never would be.

We were tangled up in this perfect moment, but it

couldn't last forever no matter how much I wanted it to. Our last time.

One more night.

I rocked desperately into her tight heat as her panting breath turned into pleading mewls in my ear. I slid my thumb against her clit—circling it once, twice—until she went off with me.

I stayed buried inside her, we were still, quiet, wrapped in each other's arms and gasping for breath.

She held me tight and kissed my cheek with a soft sigh.

I bit my lip and shut my eyes, fighting against the tears that threatened to spill over.

What the hell is wrong with me?

Gathering my wits, I asked, "Are you okay, baby? Was it too much? Too hard for you?"

Hazy eyes met mine. "No. Cade, you're perfect. I've always loved being with you."

"Good. I've never—It's never been like this with anyone but you, Charlotte. I don't even think when I'm inside you. I only feel." She tightened reflexively at my words, and I groaned before slipping out and rolling to my side.

"I know, it's the same for me. With you, sex becomes beautiful, like something out of a dream." She snuggled close, resting her head on my chest. "Will you stay with me tonight?"

"Yes." I would stay tonight. I wished I could stay every night into forever. I never wanted to leave.

It's funny how life is full of so many moments that you think are one thing but are actually something else.

One more night. The idea of it was bullshit.

This wasn't closure; I had been fooling myself. This was my heart finally accepting the truth.

I'm in love with her.

I had always loved her.

I'd never stopped.

Chapter 16
Charlotte

I awoke, afraid he would be gone.

But he wasn't.

The hard press of his body stretched out behind me while his strong arm draped across my waist, holding me close.

Content, I sighed as tears filled my eyes.

One more night.

It was already morning, the dim glow of the sun peeked through the slats of my blinds, and I wished I could go back to sleep so he couldn't leave me. I didn't want our night to end.

I had always considered myself a tough girl. I mean, I had five older brothers and I rarely cried, but I was at full emotional capacity right now.

I was about to lose my shit and cry all over Cade. And he was sweet, a good guy, the best of the best. So, he'd hold me for sure, give me all the comfort I required and more, but then he'd leave, and I'd be alone again.

I was sick and tired of being alone.

How much more was I supposed to take?

My stalker from hell?

The deadline of doom?

And now the dawning realization that I was head-over-heels, crazy in love with my ex-husband?

And he was lying behind me, poking my behind with his huge epic boner *and* we'd just spent our so-called, mother freaking last night together *and* it was pure magical heaven?

I could not handle any more of this stupid fricking nonsense life kept handing me. Not one bit.

My entire body ached from holding back the words I didn't dare say to him. Not yet, anyway. Not until I maybe finished writing my book and got my head clear of the dumbass ideas I had believed about my life over all these years away from him.

I should have come back to Sweetbriar a long time ago. I should have fought for him.

"Baby?" His arm tightened around my waist while the deep throaty groan of his sleepy morning voice shot straight to the good spot between my legs.

I couldn't help but wiggle my booty against him in response before I sat up. I turned to say good morning but ended up staring at him like a weirdo instead.

It was as though he had come straight from the pages of one of the dirty parts in my books. The sun through my window highlighted the ripple of his abs, his big arm was bent behind his head with the muscles bunched just so, and the sheet had come to rest low around his hips and pulled tight enough to outline his gorgeous, hard cock that had been poking me in the bottom only moments before.

Why in the hell did I sit up?

Damn, he was fine. He'd always been fine, but I'd forgotten how irresistibly sexy early morning Cade was. Tousled-up hair, half-mast eyes, and don't even get me started on that broad, muscled chest with the perfect amount of dark hair dusted across. I bit my lip and he smiled at me.

"Morning, Charli," he drawled, his voice like a caress on my bare skin. I shivered.

"Hi, Cade," I squeaked.

He beckoned me with one hand, crooking a finger with a naughty grin. "Get back here."

I went. I was only human. And the whole "one more night" thing was not even my idea.

He kissed me.

It lingered.

Hands on my skin.

Bodies pressed close.

My heart like a bass drum pounding in my chest beating hope throughout my veins.

Our lips pressed harder together, opening, this kiss pushing us into a future we hadn't defined. One that existed beyond the time limit we had set the night before.

Then he stopped. "I promised you French toast, but you don't have what I need so I'll owe you."

I don't have what he needs. Did I ever?

I bit the inside of my lip. Hard. "Don't worry about it.

Do you work today? Maybe we could get breakfast together?"

"I do. Yeah, I'm on duty. What time is it?"

I found my watch on the night table. "It's six."

"I overslept. I should get a move on. Can I call you later?"

"Yes. I feel like maybe we need to talk about this?"

"I agree." He smiled at me before he sat up, shifted his legs to the floor, then bent to gather his clothes and get dressed. I tugged the sheet up to cover myself and watched, dejected.

I was blue.

Beyond sad.

I wanted to bury myself under my covers and cry until I passed out and couldn't think anymore. I didn't know what to do or what I should say to him.

Fear held me back from everything I knew my heart wanted tell him. I stared at the floor. I couldn't stand to watch him leave.

He circled around the bed stopping at my side. "Hey." Lifting my chin with a fingertip he bent and kissed my forehead. "Last night was special. We'll talk about it tonight, okay? I'll call you when I get off. I promise."

"All right. Until tonight then."

I heard his footsteps down the stairs and the twist of the lock before he shut the door behind himself. He was gone.

"Crap," I whispered to no one as I fell back to the pillows and tears filled my eyes. "Damn it." Did he really have to work? I hated that I doubted his word when I never had before.

The front doorknob jiggled, and I heard a faint knocking. "Cade? Is that you? I'm coming." I wrapped the sheet around myself and flew down the stairs. I opened the door, but no one was there. It must have been the wind. I mumbled to myself, "I swear, I'm losing my damn mind," and shut the door with a slam, locked it, then set the alarm.

I needed to get some work done. But my mind was everywhere but on my manuscript. I headed to the kitchen to get the coffee started while I took a shower.

I stopped in front of the door leading into the garage. The light was on; it shone through the bottom crack of the door.

Freaking McMillon.

He had sworn he would contact me if he ever had to go into the garage. I didn't want to live in a place where I had to worry about someone coming and going and interrupting me. I liked my privacy, which was part of the reason the whole stalker situation drove me so crazy.

I opened the door, slid my hand down the wall and switched the light off in a huff. I was kind of grateful to have somewhere to focus my bad mood.

I didn't care how early it was. I shot off a text to McMillon telling him to let me know next time he had to use the garage, then stomped upstairs to get ready for my sure to be horrid day.

After my shower I flopped onto my bed to contemplate everything that had happened since I had crashed into the tree at Cade's place. I managed to get some work done, a little bit of reading, a few texts with Trent, and a lot of staring at the wall before my eyes drifted shut and I fell into what was sure to be an epic nap.

The incessant ring of my cell woke me hours later—it was Cade.

Unfortunately, I was still confused, having come to zero conclusions during my almost comatose nap. "Hello."

"Hey, I know it's after dinner time, but do you have room for sushi?"

"My body always has room for sushi, Cade. But I haven't eaten yet, so this is perfect."

"Are you still up for a talk tonight? I can pick up your favorites and we can meet at my place? In an hour?"

"Sure. I'll be there, don't forget the—"

"Rainbow roll, dragon roll, miso soup, and a Diet Coke. Unless something has changed." I swear I could hear the wink in his voice. It made me smile.

"Nope, that's it. I'll bring dessert." Before he could say anything, I continued, "Apple pie from the Sweetbriar Diner with vanilla ice cream and caramel sauce on the side. Unless something has changed, that is."

The deep sound of his laugh filled my ear. "You got it. I'll see you soon."

I swiped to end the call and sat up, horrified when I caught my reflection in the mirror above my dresser. I should have known better than to fall asleep with wet hair. Yeesh. I quickly got ready to leave.

An hour later I was at Cade's.

Two hours later we were finished with dinner and sitting on the back deck enjoying glasses of wine and the twinkling stars in the sky. A shared blanket covered our legs as we rocked in the porch swing and watched the mist rise through the forest over the mountains.

It was quiet. We had spent dinner in the kitchen making small talk and jokes, but the atmosphere out here somehow felt heavier.

He cleared his throat and took my hand. I held myself back from running away; I had to follow this through no matter how much it may end up hurting. Ever since we slept together, each moment we shared was tinged with a fragility that frightened me. It was as if we weren't moving forward but waiting for another inevitable end.

"I know," I said. "We need to talk. Don't we?"

"I don't know how to say what I need. I don't want you to take it the wrong way."

"That sounds ominous." I laughed to cover my sudden surge of nervous energy. "I guess you should just say it."

"Me and you. Can we see where this goes without defining it? I don't want—"

"You don't want to get hurt again," I deduced.

He nodded with earnest eyes. "Right, but—"

"I don't want to get hurt either, you know."

"I—yeah. It killed me when you left, Charlotte. I don't know any other way to put it. I was devastated. But that's not what I'm getting at right now—"

"It didn't have to be that way. You wanted the

divorce, I didn't." I looked away, squinting into the dark landscape of the forest.

"Look at me please." Reluctantly, I met his eyes. "You had to be free to go after what you wanted without worrying about me or where we stood. I couldn't allow myself to hold you back, and I wasn't the kind of man to wait around. You weren't the waiting type either. You can't deny it. We are both ambitious people."

"I get it." I really didn't get it. But we'd been over and over what had gone wrong between us in the past. We'd had the same conversation repeatedly back then, and it had gone nowhere. He thought he knew what was best for both of us, and I ended up being forced to abide by his decision.

But, then again, what was the point in dredging up old hurts right now when he obviously wasn't ready to move past them? "Actually, I kind of don't get it. I'm confused. Do you want me to leave you alone, Cade? Is that what you're saying?"

"No." He brushed the hair from my face, resting his palm against my cheek. "Being with you makes me feel alive again. I don't want last night to be our last time together."

I held his wrist and smiled. "I feel the same way about you."

"But I won't hold you back. You have a career you should be proud of. You have goals that lie elsewhere—"

I jerked out of his hold and stood. "This is starting to sound like ten years ago all over again. I don't understand where you're going with this. If you don't want to see me, just say it please. If we're over again, don't drag it out."

"It can be different this time. We're older now, no longer kids. We're mature adults, we can handle things now that we couldn't before."

"Okay . . ."

"What I'm saying is, whenever you come home for a visit, I want you to get off that plane and come straight to me. I want you too much to let you out of my life completely, but I won't be the one to keep you away from what you've created for yourself in New York. Do you understand now?"

"But can you live like that? You said you couldn't before. What about what you want?"

What about what I want. Do I even know what I want?

"All I can think about is you, and I'll take you however I can get you. Being with you again has made me realize that I never truly let you go. Look at my life—I'm still here, in our house. Sleeping in our old room, alone. I never moved on, not really. I was too busy being yours to fall for another woman. I can't make myself let you go; I don't even want to. But I won't ask you to stay in Sweetbriar and sacrifice your life just to be with me."

"Oh, Cade." I was floored.

"It doesn't have to hurt this time. I don't want to hurt you. I will never hurt you ever again. Do you trust me?"

"Yes. I would trust you with my life, Cade. Always."

"Be mine in Sweetbriar, Charlotte. Whenever you get into town, come to me, stay with me."

"What about when I'm not in Sweetbriar?" I murmured, not sure I liked where he was going with this, but at the same time, unwilling to risk losing him again by saying no, or asking for more than he was willing to give me.

"We won't discuss that. No questions asked. I don't want to know." He raked a hand through his hair in frustration, leaving it on the back of his neck as he looked away. "The thought of it—"

"Okay, I get it. So, we're together, I'm yours, in Sweetbriar." *What if I wanted to be his everywhere?*

"Yeah." The possessive glint of his eyes in the dark sent shivers down my spine.

"Okay." I darted my tongue out, wetting my lips in anticipation. "Yes." Being with him was all what I wanted. Did it really matter how?

"We'll start right now." He yanked me into his arms and kissed all the hesitation and doubts out of me. "You're mine, Charlotte."

"Maybe you're mine," I whispered against his lips.

"I'll be yours. I'll be anything for you."

"I don't want to lose this—whatever we have."

"We don't need anything but us." He kissed me. "My beautiful Charlotte, whenever we're together, I swear I'll make you happy."

"You already do. Being home with you was something I didn't even know I needed again. Now I don't want to live without it."

"You won't have to."

I knew better than to ask him for a promise.

There was nothing guaranteed in this life anyway.

Right then, I decided to live moment to moment instead of letting my ambitions for the future destroy my present. I already knew I couldn't have everything I wanted. No one could have it all. But I could keep what I already had safe.

Chapter 17
Cade

I used to take it for granted that I'd always wake up to see her next to me. Then I lost her and learned that there were no guarantees in this life, not even if you'd made vows and had a ring on your finger.

Her pretty face in the early morning sunlight took my breath away. I hadn't felt like this in years. She was in my bed, naked in my arms, just like hundreds of times in the past and I never wanted her to leave.

Dark eyelashes fluttered against her cheeks, and I took a deep breath as she stirred in her sleep. She was the most beautiful woman I would ever see in my life, and I would keep her in it no matter what I had to sacrifice. No more taking her for granted.

"Good morning," I whispered.

"Cade." She smiled and reached up, winding her arms around my neck. "I love waking up with you."

"I wish I didn't have to go into the station." I dipped down to kiss her forehead.

"I know, me too. Too bad we can't freeze time. I should call my publisher and work out a new deadline. I need to take control of my life again." Her eyes darted away from mine and the sense that she wasn't telling me something reignited.

"What do you mean, take control? What are you hiding, Charlotte? You know I'll do anything in my power to help you, right? Is it about the crash—"

"I just have a lot going on, is all. Kiss me."

It didn't escape my attention that she hadn't given me a real answer. But I didn't want to push, and I really wanted to kiss her, so I did.

"If you're hiding something, I'll find out eventually." I'd just keep her townhouse on the rotation. I'd had officers discretely cruising down her street a few times a day since the accident. So far, nothing out of the ordinary had been observed.

"Hmmm." She peppered kisses to my neck and upper chest. "You're not kissing me enough. I need more," she murmured, smiling as she pressed a kiss against my lips.

I flipped her to her back and gave her my full attention. "Is this what you had in mind?" I slid my fingers between her legs, and yeah, this was absolutely what she had in mind. She was ready for me. I buried myself inside her with a groan.

She wrapped her legs around my waist, and I focused on making her come rather than answering any more questions. So much for "one more night," but this was much better. I rocked into her body, again and again, determined to bring her over the edge with me.

After we finished, we laid there for a moment, tangled up together with our breath slowing and our bodies relaxing against each other. She scratched my back and kissed my cheek, her hands drifting into my hair as my body thrummed with pleasure. "Am I too heavy?" I sighed into her neck.

She held me tighter. "No, I love how you feel. I don't want to move. Why can't we just stay here in this bed? Sleeping and making love into perpetuity. We can have food delivered, and your bathroom is right there. We could shower together again! I remember the mornings we used to have. God, Cade, please tell me this will work."

"I will make it work. No matter what it takes. Don't worry."

"Okay, I won't worry. I'll trust you." She slid out of my arms, out of my bed and headed for the bathroom with a lingering look over her shoulder. I took the hint and joined her in the shower.

I made her coffee and breakfast and we talked about everything except what I really wanted to address. I kept things light, so I could keep her comfortable. I didn't want to scare her off now that I was closer to having her back in my life. And now I was dressed and standing in the doorway as she stepped off the front porch to get into her Jeep and leave.

A bolt of lightning hit me at the base of my spine, anchoring me where I stood as I watched her drive away, wishing to the depth of my soul that I had never let her slip through my fingers all those years ago. I should have gone with her, or waited for her. I should have fucking listened to her plans on how we could have worked it out back then instead of behaving like a stubborn ass.

Time waited for no one, so I headed back inside to gather my things and head into the station. On the way, I stopped at Violet's for more coffee, pleased to find Charlotte's Jeep parked right in front.

A look in the window found her in the far corner table sitting with my mother and grandmother. An involuntary smile crossed my face at the possibility that I could eventually convince her to stay here forever, that maybe we could have more someday.

"Well, hello there, Detective Caden Barrett of the Sweetbriar Police Department. How are you on this fine morning?" I turned to find the photographer with the rental car from the Holloway's a few weeks ago standing there.

"Morning," I responded. I found people were more talkative the less I said, so I kept quiet.

"I found some interesting places to photograph around here, just like you said. The Ponderosa pines in particular are grand." Who the hell was this guy? He was up to something.

My eyebrows raised. "They sure are. You should try Frog Lake. You'd like it up there."

"Maybe I will." He turned to leave.

"But first, as they say, coffee." I gestured to the door. "You should go in, let me buy you a cup. Everyone should have a proper welcome to Sweetbriar, and this is the best coffee around." I was hoping I could lift his prints off a cup.

His smarmy smile faded as his eyes narrowed on mine. "I wish I could. But I'm in a rush. Maybe next time."

"What's your name?" I held out a hand and he shook it.

"Winthrop. Howard Winthrop. I'm an attorney out of Philadelphia, just here for the rest of the month, soaking up all the fresh mountain air before I go back to the city."

"Nice to meet you, Howard Winthrop. I'm glad you're enjoying our little town. Have a great rest of your day."

"I intend to." He flicked two fingers out in a wave. "See you around."

As Winthrop left, Trevor pulled up. "That was him, wasn't it?" He stared out his window.

"Yup. I do not like him, and I don't know why yet. He raises all my hackles."

"Your instincts are always dead on. I'll tail him and try to find out where he's staying. He knows your face, so stay clear."

"Will do. I'm going inside. I'll catch up with you later." He drove off and I entered the shop.

"Hey, Vi." It was busy, well into the morning rush.

"Cade, hi! The usual?" I nodded and she waved me off. I stuffed some money in the tip jar and headed to Mom's table.

Gram waved me in. "Come here, sweetheart. We're

just visiting with Charlotte. Aren't you glad she's back in town?"

"Of course." Charlotte and I exchanged an amused glance.

"Hello, Caden." Mom stood up to kiss my cheek. "How are you today, my darling boy? I'm here, writing and *not* meddling. I think I deserve a grandchild for this. Don't you, Charli, honey?"

Charlotte opened her mouth to speak, but Gram beat her to it. "I don't know, Dahlia. Nine months of pregnancy followed by childbirth doesn't quite sound like a fair exchange for not meddling."

"Meddling is my life, as we all know. So, obviously, staying out of this situation between the two of you is very taxing for me. And babies are fun little blessings, don't you think? It might be worth your while. I throw an awesome baby shower and I'm willing to babysit at a moment's notice."

"You may not be meddling, Mother, but the art of subtlety is still lost on you." I chuckled and took a seat.

She peered at me over the frame of her glasses. "Dropping hints isn't the same as meddling, dear, everyone knows that. Is Violet coming over here with your coffee? I need to talk to her about book club. I need to know what snacks she wants me to bring."

"Oh! The buffalo chicken dip for sure, please. And I am still low-key freaking out about the whole thing." Charlotte snapped her laptop closed. "Sorry, Cade, I had to get the rest of this chapter out. Hi!"

"Good morning, baby, and no apologies needed. I'm glad Adaline is finally talking to you."

A rosy flush covered her cheeks. "Me too. She finally knows what she wants and is determined to get it. No more running away. We're kind of living the same life right now."

"That's great, honey!" Mom wrapped her arm around Charlotte in a side hug. "It's all about the characters, isn't it? Once they tell you what they require, then you're off!"

"Absolutely," Charlotte answered, her eyes on me.

"I for one can't wait for the next book." Gram said as she sipped her coffee. She patted her paperback copy of *Run for It* to emphasize her point. "This girl knows her way around a love scene. Am I right?"

Charlotte turned bright red. I'd read her books, and she sure did. Some of my favorite scenes were like reading a memory. But I decided not to reply; she was embarrassed enough already.

"Here you go!" Violet plopped into the seat next to me then slid my order across the table. "I have about five minutes before the next wave hits. You wanted to ask me something, Mom?"

"Yes. I wanted to get a snack list for book club."

"Margaritas and buffalo chicken dip? Charcuterie and wine? Canapes and cocktails? Upscale or down, Charlotte? We can do anything you want."

"What do you usually do?"

"Get collectively drunk and gossip," I answered for Violet. "Does the food really matter for that?"

"Like you don't show up all eager and raring to go for

every book club, Cade." Gram rolled her eyes as she scolded me. "You know we talk plenty about books. But we also know how to have fun. You'll be fine, Charlotte. Everyone already loves you, so don't worry."

"Gram is right, Charli. Expect to be fangirled. I gotta get back to work. Tell Mom everything you want, and we'll make it happen."

"Okay, will do." She waited until Violet was out of earshot before announcing, "I have no idea what I want."

"I'll handle everything. You just show up looking fab." Mom patted Charlotte's shoulder. "You don't need any more stress."

"You got that right. Thanks, Dahlia. I appreciate your help so much."

"Do you need to talk about anything? I'm here." I offered, hoping she'd open up about the crash.

She shot me a look and sipped her coffee. "No thanks. I'll be okay. Being here with your mom is inspiring."

"Aww, I'm here for you any time, sweetheart. I'm so glad you're back!"

"Charlotte, walk me out? I need to get going. Bye, Mom."

"Bye, sweetie!" Gram called.

"We'll watch your things, Charli."

"Thank you." She followed me out to my SUV. I had no reason to drag her out here other than I wanted to make out with her, and I also wanted my mother to continue *not meddling* in my relationship with Charlotte.

If she saw me kiss her, she'd start meddling for sure. "What's up?"

"Nothing." I spun her against the side of the door and kissed her. "I like this skirt." I ran my hand up the back of her thigh and grabbed a handful of her ass over her tights.

"Ooh!" she squealed. "I guess you're not interested in keeping things between us a secret." She laughed against my mouth and threw her arms around my neck.

I kissed her nose and grinned. "Nope, but I should stop feeling you up, even if you are wearing this conveniently long coat that hides my wandering hands." I dropped my head and kissed her neck while giving her ass one last squeeze. "I love your ass. I have always loved your ass. This ass at least sixty percent of why I married you."

"Some things never change." She giggled and tipped her head to the side, giving me more access to her neck. "And you know what neck kisses do to me, Cade, and since can't exactly go at it in the back of your SUV right now, you have to knock it off or I'm going to be hot and bothered all day."

"Maybe I want to make you miss me, Charli baby," I whispered. "Maybe I want to leave you needing me."

"Oh, you're in a naughty mood, I see." She slid her warm palm against my dick, and I grunted against her neck. "It's a good thing you parked where we can't be easily seen, or you'd have to arrest us both for indecent exposure or whatever law we're currently breaking."

"You're right. I'll get lewd and lascivious with you later in the privacy of one of our homes so I can fuck you properly." I kissed the top of her head and pulled back. "We'd better stop before I lose my mind and we end up with our pants down in the back of the cruiser."

"Good thinking." She laughed. "I'd better get back inside."

"Dinner tonight?"

"Of course. You're mine in Sweetbriar, right?" I was hers everywhere, but we had time to explore that possibility later.

"Should I pick something up after work and drop by?"

She thought for a minute. "Get the taco special at the food carts. Oh! Tell them no cheese. On anything, Cade. None. And grab a Corona, but make sure they give you some lime slices."

My lips twitched as I tried not to laugh. "Anything else?"

"Don't let them cheap out on the pico, it's essential."

"Sounds good. Until tonight, Charli." I kissed her goodbye then headed to the station. Hopefully Trevor would have some news for me.

Chapter 18
Charlotte

After dinner with Cade at the Sweetbriar Diner, I'd left for Vi's book club. Yesterday was tacos at my place, and tonight we had met in town during his dinner break. And right now, I was sitting in my second-best little black dress on the sofa in the rear of the coffee shop, sipping a martini and waiting for people to start arriving. My nerves wouldn't allow me to be late, or even on time, so I was way too early.

"This is so cool," Gwen hissed in my ear. "Is Cade coming?"

"He'll be here for a bit if he can get away for another break, maybe in an hour or so."

"Eeep! Do you think he knows Jaden Skeritt is him? I haven't had the nerve to ask him."

"Dude, shut up. No one knows about that, and don't you dare ask him about it."

Her eyes slid to the side as she shook her head. "Ooookaaay, whatever you say. It's not exactly a subtle hint. Just saying, Charlotte, he reads your books. I don't know if he's caught up though."

"Oh god. He does? You know this how?"

"Girl, where are we? Come on! Do you think this is the first time we've discussed the illustrious Keli Marlowe's work?"

I shook my head side to side, fighting the instinct to cover my ears and duck beneath the coffee table. "No one reads my books. I'm not here right now, I'm in Charlotte's happy place. I don't know what you're talking about."

"This is going to be so much fun. You're being ridiculous, Charli. You go to book signings and meet and greets all the time. What is up with you right now?"

"This is hard to explain, but I'll try. Here in Sweetbriar, I am Charlotte Keli Cassidy and everyone knows me for real. At those other signings, I am Keli Badass Marlowe, and she is quite clearly not me. I either need to go home and hide, or drink like three more of these martinis in order to cope with this. I made a huge mistake when I said I'd come here. What was I thinking?"

"No way. You'll be fine. And there is no way I'm letting you get drunk. Drunk Charlotte has zero filter and if you don't want it coming out that Jaden Skeritt is Caden Barrett and you're about to write dirty fan fiction of your own life in your next book, then you need to be sober so you can lie your ass off."

"Crap. Shoot. Frick. Why, Gwen? Why am I the way that I am?"

"What I'm about to say goes along with why you're freaking out right now—which makes total sense, by the way. Listen, you choose to live your life not thinking deeply about the things that bother you." She shrugged. "Most of the time it works for you. You write books to get your feelings out, and if someone makes you mad you kill them off. You disconnect, you put things in boxes, you compartmentalize. At some point you've got to put it all together and feel your feelings, Charlotte. It might help in situations like this."

"Ouch, Gwen. Quit being real and just pat me on the head, please. Tell me it's going to be okay."

"No, because I want you to stick around this time. You need to sort yourself out and I'm here to help. I miss you. I love you. I need my best friend back in town. And you need me too. You'll never be able to stay in Sweetbriar unless you resolve your feelings about Cade."

"Maybe you're right. But not right now, okay? I'll think about resolving stuff later. Right now I want my denial back." I brushed a tear away before it could fall and ruin my perfect makeup.

Freaking feelings.

"I'm here for you too." Violet sat across from me in a club chair and patted my knee. "Don't make her think too hard tonight, Gwen. We have time, don't we, Charlotte. Your heart is here in Sweetbriar. You brought it back with you this time."

I smiled at Vi. "Yeah, I did."

She stood and patted my head. "It's going to be okay. I love you, Charli. You're a Barrett for life." With a wink, she headed off to the front of the shop to greet the book club members as they arrived.

"Love you too," I called.

Barrett for life.

Mrs. Charlotte Keli Cassidy-Barrett. Could I really be her again?

"People are starting to arrive. Are you ready for this?"

"Heck no!" I checked the time on my cell phone then put it on the coffee table. "It's too late to cancel. I have to be okay, Gwen. Like a dumbass, I kept inviting people to come here. I can't leave."

"It's going to be fine. For real. This is your home, and you're a great writer. Everyone loves you. Do you want me to pat you on the head now?" she teased gently.

"No, you did great. I feel a bit better." I took another swig of my martini and tried to gird my loins.

"Good. Oh hey! Your brothers are here, and your dad. Brody! Over here." She waved my brother over while the rest of them took seats at a table and smiled at me.

"Oh man. No one better ask me about the love scenes in front of my dad and brothers. I swear—"

"Oh, please." She laughed. "Get ready, because it will probably be the second question. And only because no one will have the balls to lead with it."

"*Ugh.* I need another drink. Just one more."

"Go on, but be careful. Violet makes them strong. Get something to eat, too."

I filled a plate of fancy snacks at the buffet table Violet had set up, grabbed another martini from the tray, then moseyed back to my perch on the sofa.

Stacks of my books were piled on the coffee table and

a few other tables around the shop, ready for me to sign when the question-and-answer part was over.

I needed to get into character. I should have worn a suit; Keli Marlowe didn't bother with little black dresses. She was all about power suits and intimidating glam, with dark red lipstick and black framed glasses, just like Dahlia's. Like a fool, I had dressed like myself tonight and my nerves were about to send me running off into the night.

I inhaled a deep breath and cleared my mind—which was pretty easy to accomplish, since I was halfway back in my happy place trying to ignore reality.

Violet stood and held up her drink. "Let's raise our glasses and toast to the author of our favorite murder mystery series, *The Adaline Paige Files*, Miss Keli Marlowe, otherwise known as our own Charlotte Cassidy! We're so glad you're here, Charli, I mean, Miss Marlowe." She winked and beamed her gorgeous smile at me and I was grateful because her support and love was doing a lot to keep me sane right now. "Thank you for coming."

"I wouldn't miss it. I'm so happy you invited me to be here. And, in Sweetbriar I'm just Charli, like always. Let's keep it simple."

"Perfect! Let's jump right in and start with some questions."

"Oh, oh! Me! Me! Me!! I have one. I have been waiting for this." Gwen's sister, Elizabeth from the Quickbriar Stop and Go, shouted, and waved her copy of *Beg for It* over her head. Crap, that was my dirtiest book.

I ducked my chin into my chest and sank down in the sofa.

"Okay, Elizabeth, you're first!" Violet laughed as she gave her the floor.

Cade strode through the door exactly as Elizabeth stood up to ask her question. I waved him over and he smiled.

"Charli, I have to know. How do you get your ideas for all those spicy love scenes? And I want you to sign page sixty-nine of my book. Did you plan for that scene to go on that exact page, by the way? Like how?" I shot a glance to Gwen as Elizabeth pursed her lips and turned away from Gwen's angry glare.

"Your fricking sister is going in a book!" I hissed at a horrified Gwen. "Next time I'm in her store I swear I'm stealing some stuff."

Gwen shook her head. "I can't believe that girl some-times. No shame, that one. I'll talk to her."

"Dude, it's too late now. The dirty cat is out of the bag. Is my face red?" Gwen nodded.

"Don't be embarrassed because I'm here, Charlotte." My father shouted. "Your momma didn't get you and your brothers in her belly through immaculate concep-tion. Go on and answer the question." Everyone laughed. Meanwhile, I felt like at least a year had been taken off my life because I had just metaphorically died of humiliation.

"Holy fricking hell," I mumbled under my breath as I mentally forced myself back into my happy denial bubble and tried to come up with a plausible answer. "Uhhh . . ." Literally every dirty thing I had ever written about I had done with Cade, even the butt stuff. "Porn." My shoulders shrugged up and I nodded. Was that a better answer than the truth? Probably not, but I doubled down anyway. "Yeah, I just—I watched a lot of porn for inspiration."

"Moving right along!" Violet helpfully interjected. "Tell us about the new hot cop you debuted in *Ready for It*, Officer Jaden Skeritt. Is he going to be Adaline's new love interest?" Her eyes darted to Cade as he sat down next to me on the sofa, and a nervous laugh burst out of her. "Oh shit." She hiccupped and sipped her martini. "I just got that."

Gwen handed me her drink. "Chug it. I'll go get you another one. No one should be sober for this."

"You always have my back and I fricking love you for it," I said as she headed for the bar set up next to the shop's counter.

Cade looked at me with the absolute definition of "shit eating grin" unfurling across his face. He was loving this. His eyebrows shot up and his hand went to my thigh as he waited for me to answer.

"Uh, I'm a little behind on my manuscript. And as a writer who never outlines, I just don't know yet. So, um, we'll all have to wait and see." My author skills didn't include stuff like this. I could write the crap out of a fight scene and my characters could bang to everyone's satisfaction for a chapter or two, but this? This was insanity. Why wasn't there a handbook for how authors should behave in front of their readers? Someone should write one.

"What are Jaden's odds?" Cade murmured under his breath. That big hand on my thigh squeezed possessively and I gulped.

Startled, I gazed into his amused brown eyes and answered without thinking. "I'd say the odds are in Jaden's favor."

His lips tipped up at the corner and he winked. "I love this."

"I can tell."

My cell phone on the coffee table pinged with an incoming text. Cade and I both saw the message as it popped up on the screen.

Trent: Charlotte, darling, everything is fine in NY so I'm flying into Portland. I'll see you very soon. Nothing to worry about, I promise. I just miss your gorgeous face. XO

Cade's smile vanished along with his hand on my thigh. "So, I have to get back to the station, Charlotte. I'll call you soon, okay?"

"Cade, wait!" But it was too late; he was halfway across the shop, then gone. I couldn't chase after him and make a scene, could I?

"Charlotte. What's going on?" Gwen passed me another drink and sat down.

"Nothing. He had to go back to work." I took a healthy sip of the martini and tried to hold myself together as I waited for the next question.

Jaden's odds were diminishing right alongside Cade's.

How could I live like this?

Would he ever stop and listen to me? Or would he go on into infinity jumping to his own conclusions and avoiding everything I had to say?

I felt like crying but I was empty inside.

I had no more of my heart left to break, because it belonged to him again.

Chapter 19
Cade

ine in Sweetbriar meant nothing when her other ex-husband was on his way here to be with her. To be fair, it was my own damn fault for not throwing down and declaring what I wanted from the get-go. I had never been afraid to be direct with any woman—only Charlotte. I had wanted to avoid scaring her off, avoid putting too much pressure on rekindling our relationship.

Now it was coming back to bite me on the ass.

But as the only woman who held the power to hurt me, it made sense how I behaved toward her. My heart was in her hands, and it terrified me. I'd lost her once before and the thought of not having her in my life tore me up inside.

I was on duty for the rest of the night, so having a few beers at Holloway's to unwind and think this over was not something I could do right now. Instead, I headed back to the station to meet up with Trevor. Hopefully he had information on Sweetbriar's newest visitor and current thorn in my side.

I found Trevor in his office. Paperwork was the bane of our existence, and he was catching up on a mountain of it. His laptop was open, and a huge cup of coffee was in his hand.

"Hey," he greeted when he spotted me. "I thought you'd still be at Vi's. I was about to text you what I found out, which was a big nothing. I followed him to the Mountain Breeze Motel. Howard Winthrop really is an attorney from Pennsylvania. His ID checks out—clean record, owns his own home, divorced, no children, good credit. I found nothing amiss. On paper he's upstanding and his room is paid up until the end of the week."

"Damn it. I—"

"Hey, I get it. If he's hiding something, we'll just have to wait until whatever it is plays out. Don't stop trusting your gut. Your instincts have never been wrong."

"Thanks, man. I still want to keep an eye on him. Something is off, I just know it. And let's keep Charlotte on our radar too. She's not telling me something, and I have a bad feeling about it." What I couldn't get a handle on was where these suspicions were coming from.

I was frustrated that my logic was clouded by her presence. I couldn't seem to see past my fear of potential heartbreak. Was the bad feeling due to Trent and her relationship with him? Was that what she was hiding from me? Was it simply jealousy I felt, or something more?

"How are things going with her?" Trevor interrupted my spiraling thoughts, and I was grateful.

"Her ex-husband—the other one—is coming for a visit." I sat in the chair across from his desk.

"Shit. I'm sorry, man."

"I was at Vi's book club and a text popped up on Charlotte's phone. He called her 'darling'. I read it and just got up and left. I told her I had to go back to work. I feel like an ass, but I—"

"I mean, you did have to come back here tonight, so that's not a lie. But you didn't at least let her explain first?"

I shook my head. I had definitely messed up tonight. "Well, it was in the middle of the Q and A, and it was crowded. I couldn't exactly have a deep conversation at that point—"

"That makes sense. But you need to talk about this stuff with her, Cade. Quit reacting and running."

"You're probably right," I hedged.

"I'm totally right." His smile was understanding. "I almost lost your sister because I was a stubborn fool. Keeping your feelings to yourself is never a good idea. It's like putting off the inevitable. You should know this. You were there for the worst of what happened between Rose and me."

"Yeah, and I'm still sorry for punching you." At one point, he'd broken up with her for what he thought was her own good. Rose was devastated, and in classic big brotherly fashion, I took it out all over his face.

"Don't be." He chuckled. "You knocked the sense back into me and it all worked out in the end, didn't it?"

"Sure did."

"Want to grab a drink at Holloway's after shift? I'm buying. The kids are at my parent's place for the night. And Rose is at book club, of course. She's staying to help Vi clean up after."

"I should probably try to get ahold of Charlotte and apologize for running out on her."

"Rose said she's sticking around the shop after it ends too."

"Sounds good. Then I'll catch up with her after, or tomorrow morning first thing, if it runs late."

"Good. Be proactive and send flowers. That sort of worked for me with Rose."

"Good idea." I pulled up the Sweetbriar flower shop's website on my phone and placed an order to arrive in the morning. "I don't want to interrupt her again, anyway. They were asking her some pretty intense questions that I don't think I want to be around for. I got the sense that me being there was making it worse for her. Which reminds me, I need to read the latest *Adaline* book. I guess there's a new character sort of named after me. She wouldn't really do that . . . would she?"

"According to Rose, yes she would."

I grinned. "I need to dig up my copy and read it for myself."

"Maybe it will give you a clue, detective." His smirk was only sort of infuriating since I deserved it.

"I guess it's my turn to take all the shit."

"Now that you put it that way, I'll try to come up with more to bust your chops with."

"Thanks a lot—"

My dad at the door interrupted us. "I need you both to head to the hospital. Old man McMillon was just held up in his house. He's hurt and shaken up, but he'll pull through."

"Shit, that's terrible. He's got to be at least eighty years old," Trevor remarked as he stood.

"As horrible as that is, it's not the worst part." Dad's face was stone. "Whoever it was took his phone, laptop, and the keys to all his properties. It's all hands on deck tonight. I don't want anyone else getting hurt because of this."

"Damn." I was glad I'd already put Charlotte on our radar. But I'd check on her myself tonight to be sure.

"We got this. Let's head out. Meet you there." Trevor took off, but I lingered to ask my dad a few more questions.

"Do you think this could have anything to do with Charlotte and the crash?" There was no logical reason for me to tie the two events together. Bethany Rhodes had been in the other car and she definitely had nothing to do with what had happened tonight—I had seen her lurking at Violet's book club, and no one could be in two places at once—but my mind still wouldn't let it go.

"I don't see how. But it wouldn't hurt to keep an eye on her. She's with Vi at the shop now. If it's like every other book club meeting they've ever had, they'll go for a few more hours at least. She'll be fine while she's there.

Are Matt and Quinn still doing extra patrol on her street?"

"Yes."

"Good. McMillon owns those townhouses, so I'll add a few more cars to the area. I'll shoot a text to her dad, too. She should go home with him for the night, just to be safe."

"Good. Thanks. I'll head out now."

"Careful, son."

"Always."

I met Trevor in McMillon's room. The grouchy old man was beat up and pissed off. He pointed a crooked finger at me as I approached his bed. "Good, you're here too. I want you to catch that jerk immediately. He took my keys and all the information on my rentals. I can't have my tenants getting messed with. Do you know what that will do to my reputation? I got three vacant properties to fill!"

"Your reputation?" I was aghast. "What about the safety of your tenants?"

"What about it? Who cares! Just catch that asshole and do it fast. I want it done tonight."

He was unbelievable. Charlotte needed to find a new place to live. "You won't have to worry too much about the townhouses on Pine, right? If someone tries to get into one of those, they'll probably slide all over the mossy front porches and cause a ruckus. Plenty of warning for whoever is inside."

He glared at me for a moment then looked away.

"Let's get out of here." Trevor was as disgusted as I

was. "He didn't see anything. He was jumped from behind."

I nodded, ready to get out of here and find this guy.

"An officer will be standing outside your door all night." Trevor informed McMillon. "You'll be safe, okay?"

He grumbled, "Yeah, fine," and switched on the television. "Send a nurse in here when you leave. I need some food."

"Sure thing." I exchanged a glance with Trevor before he turned to leave. "Get some rest, Mr. McMillon."

"Catch that bastard!" he shouted at our backs as we left.

As we headed out of the hospital, Trevor grumbled, "What a prick."

"Yeah, he's always been that way. So, we're basically just cruising around looking for anything out of the ordinary. This should be easy," I deadpanned.

"Matt and Quinn are at McMillon's trying to lift prints, but no luck so far. The only thing McMillon remembered was the thick leather gloves the suspect was wearing."

"Great. I know where I'm going to start."

"Meet you at the Mountain Breeze to check on our new friend, Howard Winthrop?" He chuckled.

"You got it."

We got into our respective vehicles and left.

Winthrop's rental wasn't parked in front of his room and the lights were off. Nothing about that was against the law. I had no reason to put out the call to find him and I would not abuse my position and malign his name in such a way without probable cause.

"Damn it." I waved Trevor off and took off behind him with the feeling I was missing something.

And that Charlotte held the key.

Chapter 20
Charlotte

Adaline crept across the dark expanse of her living room on her way to confront the shadowy figure who had taken up residence on her sofa. "Jaden," she whispered. "I told you I'd be fine. You can leave."

"I'm staying right here until I know for sure you'll be safe." The deep growl in his voice sent a thrill through her body and she shivered. "He'll have to go through me to get to you, Adaline." His words were a vow. She knew he would stay no matter what she said to him, the stubborn man.

"Fine. Have it your way. I'm going to sleep." Her heart pounded as she spun on her heel to go back to bed.

"Good night, Addie baby." His eyes were on her; she could feel the heady weight of his gaze on her body as she walked away, and it took everything she had not to beg him to join her . . .

Windchimes . . .

Windchimes . . .

WINDCHIMES!

"Damn it, damn it, damn it!" I yelled and shut my laptop with an angry slam.

Along with my deadline, my stalker, and the many intrusive questions thrown my way earlier tonight, insomnia had always been my nemesis.

I was up in the middle of the damn fricking night, sitting on my couch, covered with a blanket, trying to finish writing the chapter I'd been stuck on for weeks. I was having no luck because I seemed to have acquired a new nemesis tonight; the dang, stupid windchimes Gwen had given me were out there blowing in the breeze and driving me to the brink of insanity.

I flopped back on the couch as my mind drifted back to Cade and how he had rushed off after the text from Trent and I cursed again.

After four martinis, two fancy snacky plates, a bazillion questions about Adaline, and a healthy amount of embarrassment, Violet's book club was over. After everyone left, I had helped Cade's sisters clean up the shop and secretly hoped they'd all be my sisters-in-law again. Once I explained my relationship with Trent to Cade, he'd understand, and we could go back to muddling our way toward our second chance.

The windchimes clanged together again and I kicked my legs on the couch like an angry toddler.

"Damn it, Gwen. Damn it, crap." I was thinking about her exactly like she said I would, but it was only ten percent fondly. The other ninety percent of her was going to get an earful in the morning, ten minutes before her wake-up time. I knew her alarm went off at six every morning. She'd be hearing from me at five-fifty. Revenge was a dish best served cold—and at the crack of dawn.

I should be asleep right now. Or at least getting some good work in, but noooooo. I was in the middle of an exhausted, semi-drunken rage fest, and all bets were off as complicated payback plans rushed through my mind.

With a violent toss of the afghan on my lap, I got up, slid my feet into my slippers, and stomped across the house toward the front door. Those windchimes were history.

"Freakin' noisy piece of crap," I muttered as I began to cross the porch, sliding over the slick deck, still wet with rain from earlier this evening. "Damn it! Shoot!" I made it to the edge, grabbing onto the railing for balance with my feet almost sliding out from under me as I reached toward the wind chimes—which were hanging there quiet and still. "What the—?"

My eyes ran over the front yard, gliding slowly over the silent dark of the night as goosebumps rose over my flesh.

The garage door was open.

The air was cold and still.

There was no wind.

My blood turned to ice as I stupidly froze in place.

I'd written creepy stuff exactly like this in my books. I should have known better than to go outside.

Never, ever freaking go outside!

"Adaline." A deep voice in the darkness scared the ever-loving hell out of me and I jumped.

"Holy crap!" I stepped back with a lurch, clutching the windchimes in my fist, twisting as I slipped on the slick surface of the porch and tumbled down, hitting my cheekbone on the side of the Adirondack chair across from the open front door.

Pain radiated through my face, stunning me. I let the windchimes fall to the deck and covered my pounding cheek with my hand. It was bleeding.

I peered into the black night beyond my porch and saw the dark outline of a man. I couldn't quite make out who it was, but I knew it was *him*. My stalker had always addressed me as Adaline in the letters he'd sent, and he'd always kept a bit of distance from me, just like this. I'd never seen him up close.

"Don't be scared, darlin'. It's only me, your beloved husband, and I would never, ever hurt you. But we do need to talk a few things over, you hear? I forgave you the first two times, Adaline. I heard you fucking him right in there on the staircase inside our home. I heard your plea-sured cries. Don't deny what you were doing with him. Those are sounds that only I should hear, my Adaline. I tried to forget about it—truly, I did. But then I heard rumblings around town that you are getting back together with him. People talk about you, and I don't like what they have to say."

"I don't know what you're talking about. Who?" My

feet and hands slid around on the mossy deck as I tried to scramble toward the open doorway to get away from him.

"You and Jaden. Look at me Adaline! I'm not dead." I heard it when his hand hit his chest for emphasis. He was agitated and shouting now, and I was terrified out of my mind. "I'm here. It's me, your Tim. And all this means you're cheating on me, and we can't have that. No, we cannot. Adaline would never cheat on her beloved Tim. My Adaline is no whore, and you're going to have to fix everything in our next book. You're going to make it all go away. Erase what you did so we can be happy again. Back to the way things were."

"No! Stay away from me!"

"You need a reminder, Adaline. You forgot who you belong to." He advanced toward the porch, but I managed to crawl inside the front door and slam it before he got close enough to touch me.

"Oh god, oh god . . ." I stood and locked it. I ran across my living room and fumbled for my cell phone on the coffee table, dialing for help while frantically trying to remember where I put my purse. "Hurry, hurry, hurry."

"Nine-one-one, what is your emergency?"

"I need help. Someone's here—"

He pounded on my door. Then he kicked it and I shrieked.

"He's on my porch, trying to get inside!" I heard the knob jiggle and keys clinking together. Icy cold panic shot through my system, and I darted up the stairs into my room, locking it behind myself before tripping into my closet and slamming the door. "Please, I need help." My purse was on top of the dresser inside the walk-in closet, thank god.

"Is that you, Charlotte? Charlotte Michelle Cassidy?"

"What? Yes, that's me." I dug through my purse and found the pepper spray and the taser. I clutched the taser in my hand and tried to focus enough to tell her where I was.

"822 Pine Street, is that correct?"

"Yes, please hurry—"

"Stay on the line with me, honey. Cade and Trevor are on the way. They'll be with you in less than five minutes. They were on a case nearby. This is Doris Baumgarten from the Sweetbriar High cafeteria, remember me, sugar?"

"Oh my gosh. Yes, I remember you, Mrs. B." My voiced quivered as I fought back tears. "I'm so scared, please help me."

"Oh, my sweet girl, I know. Stay with me. Stay on the line and don't you worry about a thing. They're almost there, listen for the door. They'll shout loud to identify themselves and I'll tell you when they arrive too. Stay on the phone with me, honey. I got you."

The tears I'd been fighting filled my eyes, mixing with the blood and stinging the cut on my cheek as they fell. "Ouch, my cheek. Okay. I'm holding on."

"Good, you're gonna be just fine, sweetie. Can you hear the sirens?"

"Yes," I breathed. It sounded like a lot of vehicles were arriving, not just Cade and Trevor in the SUV.

"That's them, along with Matt and Quinn in their squad cars. They're coming to help you."

The sudden banging on the door made me jump, and I screamed. "Oh no!"

"They're on your porch, honey. I promise you it's them and that you're safe now. It's okay to go to the door."

"Charlotte, open up! It's Cade!"

"They're here. You're right it's them." But panic kept me still. I sat there petrified, trying to catch my breath.

"Stay on the line with me while you answer the door. Go on now, sweetheart, I'm here."

"Okay." I crawled out of the closet, tiptoed through my room and down the stairs to the front door, and peeked through the peep hole to find Cade and Trevor standing there. Cade's SUV and two patrol cars were parked at the curb, lights flashing. "I see them. I'm really going to be okay."

"I'm going to let you go now, honey."

"Thank you, Mrs. B. I'm so glad it was you who answered."

"Goodbye, sweetie. I'll bring you some of my strawberry muffins in the morning." She hung up.

I tossed my purse to the floor and threw open the door. Lights flashed from the squad cars parked at the curb, blinding me. "That was Mrs. B. on the phone, on nine-one-one, from the cafeteria at school. Remember her? She always used to give me an extra tapioca pudding cup at lunch because only me and your cousin

Savannah liked them. Oh my god, Cade, I was so scared."

He didn't answer me; didn't move. He was seething, his chest rising and falling with barely suppressed rage as he looked me over. I'd never seen him like this. Nervously, I swiped at my cheek. It was still bleeding a little bit, and it stung.

"What happened, Charlotte?" Trevor finally asked. "Matt and Quinn are circling the perimeter of your place. They're about to start moving up and down the streets. They called for more backup. Did you get a look at who was here? A description would be very helpful right now."

My hands still shook. "No, I didn't see him clearly—"

My eyes got big as Cade stepped closer. I trembled as he swept a gentle fingertip beneath my chin to study my face, lifting it into the light and tilting it side to side. His eyes glinted with anger in the glare of the porch lamp. It was all I could do not to throw myself into his arms.

"Tell me who hurt you, Charlotte. Who did this?" He turned my injured cheek to the side, examining my wound, his soft touch belying the fury in his words, and I trembled. All I wanted was for him to hold me.

"She might need stitches," Trevor observed.

Cade grunted his response.

Trevor gestured toward the mess of vehicles parked in front of my house. "I'll get the first aid kit. Do you want an ambulance, Charlotte? A ride to the hospital?" he offered.

"What?" As his words registered, I shook my head.

"No. I'm fine now that you're all here. I don't need an ambulance."

"You had an intruder? This wasn't random. You know something, don't you? Tell me everything Charli," Cade coaxed as he finally pulled me gently into the safety of his arms.

"Okay." I took a deep breath as I clutched at his jacket, finally able to settle my nerves a bit. "The wind chimes were making noise, so I came out here. But there was no wind. Then I noticed the garage door was open. I don't use it. My landlord keeps stuff stored in there—oh, I told you all that already. I'm sorry, I can't think! Anyway, it's supposed to be locked. And then someone said 'Adaline.' I mean, it was him. He called me that, then he started talking nonsense—"

"And your face?" Cade interrupted, pulling away to brush my hair out of my eyes and cradle my aching cheek in his broad palm.

"I fell when I was backing away from him. I slipped on the deck and hit my face there." I gestured to the chair, where some of my blood was on the corner of the armrest. *Ew.* "No one actually hurt me. It was all my own clumsy fault."

"It wasn't your fault. You wouldn't have come out onto the wet porch in the dark if someone hadn't been messing with your wind chimes to lure you outside, right?"

"I guess so."

"Quit blaming yourself for things that are not within your control, Charlotte."

"Okay, Cade. You're right." We stepped away from each other as Trevor arrived with a massive first aid kit and passed it to Cade. They exchanged a look while avoiding my eyes.

Cade removed some gauze and pressed it to my cheek.

Trevor's eyes were grim. "Take her to your place, or to her family or to the hospital for stitches. No one is going inside that house."

"What?" I breathed out, shocked. "But I'm in my pajamas—"

"Matt just informed me that it appears someone has been living in your garage. We need to search your house, dust for prints—"

"Noooooo . . ." I thought of all the things I assumed I'd misplaced over the last couple weeks due to stress or being tired. "Ohhhhh my god, oh, no no no. I'm so stupid."

"We're going to the hospital." Cade removed his coat and slipped it around my shoulders. "I've got you, Charlotte. I won't let anyone hurt you. Do you understand what I'm telling you?"

"Yeah. Okay, yes, I understand." Slowly my senses were coming back to me. "I need to make a call." I clutched my cell in the pocket of my pajama pants.

"Press the gauze to your cheek, Charli. Don't let go of it. I'm going to take you to the hospital to get this taken care of."

"Okay." He took his hand away and I pressed my fingertips to the cut. It hurt.

What was happening in New York?

Was Trent okay?

"Can I get my purse? I left it by the door when I came downstairs, it's right inside. I need to call Trent. I have to find out what—"

Cade's jaw ticked as he looked away from me. "You can call whoever you need to once we get to the hospital," he bit out.

"Right." I shivered in the cold and looked down. "Oh, my feet are gross. I don't have any shoes. Where did my slippers go?" I must have left them upstairs in the closet.

He swept me into his arms and carried me to his police SUV. Trevor followed behind with my purse and opened the door. "You're going to be okay, Charlotte. We're going to make sure of it." Cade bent and set me on the seat while Trevor turned to walk away.

I had to stop him. I had to come clean.

"Trevor, wait. Cade! Oh god. I, um. I have a stalker. His name is Douglas Winthrop. I left New York to get away from him. I have a restraining order—"

"Damn it, Charlotte!" Cade bit out and I flinched.

"Cade, take it down a notch." Trevor's voice was soothing as he tried to calm us both down. "Do you want me to drive her to the hospital?"

"No. You find this Winthrop guy. You take the lead on this. If I find him, I'll fucking kill him. I need to stay far away from this case. I can't be the one, Trevor."

"Yeah, okay. I think that's for the best. Charlotte, do you want an ambulance? Or for us to call your father? Or

Dahlia? Or I could drive you myself." Trevor's eyes darted to Cade then back to me.

"No, I'll be fine with Cade." He wasn't angry with me. I knew it because I knew him. He was frustrated and protective and he cared about me, and he had also sensed all along that I had been hiding something from him. This had to be driving him crazy. "Thank you, Trevor. I appreciate you helping me."

"It's okay, honey. Try not to worry. We got this. You'll be safe with Cade."

"I know I will. I'll be all right."

"But before I get back out there, are you familiar with a man named Howard Winthrop?"

"What? No. My stalker's name is Douglas Winthrop. It's in the restraining order and police reports in New York."

"Maybe a brother or a cousin?" he suggested.

"I have no idea. I, um, after it happened, I mean, after he appeared in person rather than just sending me letters, I called the police and got the restraining order. My friend Trent has been keeping an eye on him and as far as I know, he's been in New York this whole time. I thought everything was okay . . ." Tears filled my eyes as my words trailed off. I had no idea what to say or what was going on anymore, and where in the hell was Trent?

"The crash," Cade burst out.

"What?"

"You thought it was him following you that morning? Is that right?"

"Yeah, but it wasn't him. Also, later that day, Trent

spotted him at the McDonald's near his apartment in New York and we found out it was Bethany Rhodes who was behind me. So, it couldn't have been him that morning."

"I'll get in contact with the NYPD and go from there." Trevor interjected. "Meanwhile, we're all on overtime. We'll catch him, Charlotte. What does he look like? Was he threatening? Could you tell if he was armed tonight? Did he ever hurt you in New York?"

I told Trevor and Cade everything I knew about tonight and what he looked like and what he had done in New York. "I'm so sorry. I should have said something when I first got back to Sweetbriar, but all I wanted was to feel normal again. I just wanted my life back."

"None of that. No apologies." Trevor's voice was soothing as he tried to calm me down. "We work forward from now on, all right? If you think of anything else, tell Cade. Or text me." Trevor passed me his card. I had Rose's number but not his. "Cade, let me know if something comes up. If you think of anything else, Charlotte, please let me or Cade know. I'm out."

I felt terrible. I had put people in danger.

Cade circled around to the driver's seat and started the car to drive me to the hospital.

"Why weren't you at your dad's place? Trevor texted him earlier to take you home."

"I don't know anything about that. But my dad never has his phone. He probably left it at home. I'm really sorry."

"Don't be sorry, baby. All I care about is that you're

okay. And safe. I'm not letting you out of my sight until Winthrop is caught—Douglas *and* Howard, because they both have some questions to answer."

I leaned my head against the side window and watched the streetlights flash in the window as Cade drove.

I couldn't think anymore.

Cade reached across the console and gripped my thigh. His warm palm was comforting, I covered it with my trembling hand and held on to him.

As long as he was with me, I would be safe.

Chapter 21
Cade

I stood outside the curtain while Charlotte was being examined. I had called her dad on their landline at home while they settled her into a bed. He was on the way, along with her brothers. Lord help either one of the Winthrops if they dared to show their faces in front of her family. I halfway hoped he would show up so I could walk away and let whatever happened happen. But my father had taught me better than that; if I wanted to represent this town as its Chief of Police, I had to go by the book just like he did. Always and for everyone, not just when it was convenient. I believed that too, which is why I stepped back and wasn't out hunting Winthrop myself. I was too close to be objective and too angry to be fair.

"Where is she?" Footsteps pounded on the white linoleum as her family bounded through the emergency room doors. "Cade, where's my baby girl?" her father shouted.

"Through the curtains. She's going to be okay. They're checking her out right now."

"What happened? Who hurt her? And where the fuck is he?" His voice was a low, dangerous growl. Mr. Cassidy was a sweet man. A gentle giant. But nothing about him was gentle right now. He looked as if he wanted to tear Winthrop apart with his bare hands.

It was exactly how I was feeling inside.

"Give us a name, Cade," Hunter, the oldest, demanded.

"I can't do that, and you know it."

"She'll tell us," Brody gritted out through clenched teeth. His fists were balled at his sides, and he looked ready to punch a hole in something. Or someone.

"Every officer in Sweetbriar is out hunting him down. He'll pay. But it's going to be done the right way."

"Fuck that. That's our baby sister in there—" Tucker bit out.

"Hush, you guys, I'm fine, okay?" Charlotte's voice ringing out behind the curtain only added fuel to their ire.

"Tell us who did this, Charli. Let us take care of him for you." Spencer placed a hand on the curtain to pull it back, but I knocked it aside.

"Give her some privacy. She's shaken up, let her tell you when you can see her."

"Right. Sorry Charlotte," he called out.

The doctor popped her head between the curtains. "She's fine. I've cleaned and bandaged her cheek, and I'm just finishing up the exam right now. The plastic surgeon will stitch her up momentarily. Go to the waiting room on the fourth floor. Dr. Weaver will come out and let you know when you can go back and be with Charlotte. Except you, Detective. I understand she was attacked, and she informed me that you are her protection. Everyone else, settle down. She's upset enough."

"Fine," her dad grumbled. "Boys, come on." They formed an angry line behind their father and followed him out of the ER.

"Cade?" I peeked inside the curtain and Charlotte waved me toward her bed. "Crisis averted?" she asked.

"Yeah, they're gone."

"Good. I don't want them getting into trouble. You either, for that matter."

"That's why I put Trevor in charge. I can't stand this. He hurt you. He scared you. How long have you been keeping this to yourself, Charli? I could have made you safe a long time ago if you'd only told me."

"I'm so sorry, Cade. I should have said something. But I liked being normal again. I felt safe here and I wanted to keep that feeling. I have no good excuse."

"I let my feelings for you outweigh my suspicions that you were hiding something about the crash. I ignored my instincts and let my questions fall to the wayside in order to be with you. This is my fault."

"Hey, it is in no way your fault. This is solely on me."

"I should have made you tell me the truth."

"You can't make me do anything." She laughed, then flinched and placed her hand to her cheek. "No one can. I always do what I want."

"I bet I could have persuaded you." I winked, trying to tease her and lighten her spirits.

"Huh, maybe." She blushed. "I honestly thought I would be okay. He freaked me out in an I'm-going-to-have-to-learn-Krav Maga-and-maybe-kick-his-ass someday kind of way. Not in a stabby, murder, death, kill kind of way. Nothing like what I write in my books. Know what I mean?"

I nodded, encouraging her to go on

"He wrote letters and left comments on my social media, stuff like that. I didn't think he would hurt me. If I had, I would have never kept it a secret. He was annoying, you know? A semi-scary pest. He didn't get all terrifying and threatening and murdery until tonight. And I had no idea he thought he was Tim. That's super gross and inappropriate. I thought he was lost in the stories and thought since I wrote them, I was Adaline. Not in a sick, perverted fantasy way, but a more innocent, blurring lines of reality type of way. At least that's what his letters and comments felt like. God, I don't even know what to think anymore—"

A nurse interrupted us with a smile. "I'm going to take you up to plastic surgery now, Miss Cassidy."

Charlotte looked nervous.

"I'm right behind you Charli baby, and your family is up there already." I patted her knee and tried to soothe her. I vowed to myself that I would make her feel safe again.

She took a deep breath as her fingertips drifted across her bandaged cheek. "All right, I guess I'm ready." She paused, and looked at me, panic visible in her eyes. "Um, no, I'm not ready yet. You know how I feel about needles, Cade." She addressed the nurse. "Can you knock me out? Put me under until you're done?"

"I'm sorry, sweetheart. But no, we can't do that. Dr. Weaver is wonderful. She's fast and the best at what she does. You won't feel much, and she won't leave a scar."

"All right." After inhaling a huge sigh, Charlotte sat in the wheelchair. "Let's go."

Minutes later, I was waiting in the hall outside her door while the nurse prepped her for the stitches.

"Caden Barrett." An angry voice startled me, and I turned around.

I recognized him immediately, especially after seeing his face on the entertainment segment on the news the other night with Charlotte. It was Trent. Still, I played dumb. "Do I know you?"

"We have an ex-wife in common. My name is Trent Bishop, and I should make you suffer for being a blind idiot. I should let you go on thinking the worst about me and Charlotte, so you could finally get a taste of how much you hurt her when you let her go all those years ago. But I won't, because she's my best friend in the world and I love her."

His words didn't register. All I felt was jealousy. It hurt, and shamefully, it made me want to hurt him. "Will you be staying at her place?"

He held out a hand and scoffed. "Is that all you can think about? Obviously, you haven't changed much, or you'd already know everything about me and Charlotte, you stubborn ass. Just shut up and listen."

Who the hell did he think he was talking to me like that? "Now hold on just a minute—"

"No, *you* hold on a minute. Listen to me—just listen. First, we're going to talk about the stalker. Have you caught him?"

"No, not yet. Every cop in town is out looking."

"Damn. I called and talked to Detective Hale—Trevor—when I landed and told him everything I know. Charlotte gave me his number."

"Good. Perfect," I bit out.

"Now to ease your mind, because I know this has to be bothering you. And I'm sorry for coming at you like an asshole, but she's my best friend and you've been giving her a hard time and I don't like that. Charlotte and I are strictly platonic and always have been. *Always.* She was kind enough to marry me because I needed a wife for a year. We lived in separate bedrooms, but she helped me put on a show in public because I come from a rich family full of stuffy snobs who needed to see me acting how they thought I should."

I didn't like the sound of that. No one should feel oppressed by their own family. "And how were you supposed to act?"

"I write plays. I didn't go into the family business like the rest of them, and they can't stand it. They also like it when I have a girlfriend much better than when I bring a boyfriend around, but I like what I like, and I do what I want."

"So you and Charlotte never—?"

"I'm not going to lie and tell you that I was never interested in Charlotte because I was. She's stunning and brilliant and hilarious and she could have had me with the snap of a finger, but it became clear almost immediately that she already had a 'one and only' and that person was you. So instead, I backed off and she became the best friend I will ever have in my life." His voice dropped and he took a step closer. "And if you hurt her again, please do not underestimate what I will do for her. Do you understand?"

"I think I'm getting the picture."

"You left her at that book club. Did you even bother to think about how it would make her feel?"

"How do you even know about that?"

He held up his phone. "I've been texting with her for the last twenty minutes or so while she was in the ER being patched up, and you were waiting by the curtain. I came straight here from the airport. She's trying to play it off and not make you look bad, but I'm reading between the lines."

"I'd already planned on apologizing for how I acted, for not listening to her. I ordered flowers—"

"Uh-uh. No. I hope you know how to grovel, my friend. Because I'm not going to encourage her to forgive you until I see the flowers for myself. They'd better be expensive, flawless, and a lot of them. She'll tell me everything and she'd better be repeating some seriously romantic shit. Do you get me, Cade?"

"Yeah, I got it. I have no problem admitting when I'm wrong. She knows that."

"Good. I'm glad to hear it. I think she's also going to need some new jewelry. She's fond of silver necklaces with silly little charms. Hopefully you remember that, because it hasn't changed."

"Yeah, I remember."

"And if you get lucky enough to reach the point where you want to propose to her again, I expect to see a new ring on her finger, not that old one she wears on a chain. She's developed a taste for emerald cut. Look at her earrings next time you get in close, and you'll see what I mean. I got them for her birthday after I got my inheritance. And listen close, because this is the most important part—I'm a great friend and I'll always be in her life. You're going to have to do a lot to top me, because I'm not going anywhere and birthdays and holidays are my favorite." He smirked, effectively breaking the ice between us.

I shook my head to clear it. He'd just dumped a ton of information on me, and this night had been trying to say the least. "Look, I'm getting the sense that I was wrong about you, and I would never attempt to choose her friends for her. Or tell her to cut anyone out of her life. I'm not that type of man—"

He stopped me. "I know what type of man you are." His voice was kind when he said, "You encouraged her to follow her dreams at your own expense. You could have put the pressure on for her to stay here, but you didn't. And you could have gone with her to New York but that would have been sacrificing what you thought your own dreams were. You know better now what your dream really is, I suspect. Don't you?"

"How do you know so much?"

"Obviously, she tells me everything. But honestly, she wouldn't still love you if you weren't worth it. Charlotte is much too smart for that, even if she doesn't realize it."

She loved me?

My heart stuttered, then raced out of control. I had no idea what to say to him. "Well, okay then. I'm glad to finally meet you, Trent."

"Likewise. Don't worry, the two of us will be friends soon enough."

I chuckled. "You know what? I believe we will." I had the feeling he always got his way.

He held out a hand and I shook it.

Trent sighed. "Now, back to old Douggie boy." He shook his head. "He gave me the slip. I would swear on every Bible in the world that I saw him get on a plane to Hawaii, but somehow, he ended up here and I'm not sure how that happened."

"I think he has a brother who may have been helping him out somehow. On purpose or not, I do not know."

"I've been keeping an eye on him in New York, making sure he went to work, things like that. But I'm no pro and I told Charlotte that. She insisted that she'd be safe here and if worse came to worse, she'd tell you everything."

"Well, it's worse and now she's here in the hospital getting stitches and I have every cop in town hunting for

Winthrop. As for which Winthrop they'll find, I have no idea."

"Don't let her out of your sight."

"I don't plan on it."

"That's all I care about. I want her to be safe. That nut job will pop up soon enough on his own. Her dad and brothers are great and would die protecting her, but you're a pro. I think she should stay with you."

"I agree."

"Great. I'll help convince her if she puts up a fight."

"She won't."

His lips tipped up at the corner. "Little bit smug, aren't you?"

I shrugged. Confident and smug were not the same. Charlotte belonged with me. She'd see it too. It was just a matter of time.

Dr. Weaver stepped out. "I'm going to the waiting room to talk to her family. She's asking for you, Detective Barrett. She can go home whenever she's ready."

"Thank you." I headed through the door with Trent following behind me. "How are you feeling?"

"Better, thank you. Trent! I told you to wait. I haven't had a chance to explain—"

"It's taken care of," he replied. "No worries. We're good, aren't we, Cade?"

"All good," I confirmed.

Charlotte's nose wrinkled up in doubt. "Really?"

"Yes," I told her. "And even if we weren't good, we both care about you too much to make this awkward right now. Keeping you safe is all that matters."

"Exactly." Trent took her hand with a gentle smile. "But I explained everything about me and you. We talked it all over, and Charli, I think you need to go home with Cade."

She shook her head. "No, it's fine, my dad is here. He'll take me home. I'll be okay at the house with him and my brothers—"

"Nope, no way." Mr. Cassidy strode through the door and straight to Charlotte with her brothers hot on his heels. "We agree with Trent. You're going to Cade's. If you're not comfortable with that, we'll go with you. You need professional protection. And I am not about to try to manage your safety along with keeping your hot-headed brothers out of trouble. This situation is out of hand. I can't believe you didn't tell us what was going on with you, Charli! But that's a discussion for another time. I love you, my baby girl. You scared the absolute hell out of me." He pulled her into his massive arms, while her brothers surrounded her bed.

"I'm sorry, Dad," she mumbled into his chest. "I don't know what to say."

"There's nothing you need to say, princess, and no need to apologize. We're all just glad you're going to be okay and that this is all out in the open so we can fix it for you."

"We still need his name," Hunter grumbled. "I'll fix it real quick."

"You're not getting one. Not yet anyway," I argued.

His jaw ticked with grudging understanding. "You're

probably right. I hate this. Charli, please tell me you're going to be all right."

"I'll be fine, you guys. I promise." Her voice trembled as she held on to her dad.

"I hate it too," I said. "That's why I'm here at the hospital and Trevor is lead on this case. I'll tear him apart if I catch him."

"You guys don't have to come to Cade's," Charlotte interjected. "I mean, is it even okay that I stay at your place? I don't want to impose."

I stifled a laugh. "Honestly, I was going to take you home with me whether you liked it or not. This works out much better."

"Oh," a nervous laugh fluttered out and her cheeks colored red. "Okay. Thank you. Good thing I'm not in the mood to argue with anyone. All I want to do is get some sleep and forget everything for a while."

"I'll go pull my car around to the exit. If all of you stay with her, she'll be okay for a few minutes."

I shot Trevor a text on the way to the parking lot.

He responded immediately. No news. They were still looking.

Chapter 22
Charlotte

"**N**one of you say a word, please. I feel bad enough and I'm sorry I didn't tell you. I know I should have." I felt terrible. They were all so worried. Tucker was all welled up and trying not to cry. If he cried, I'd start crying and if I cried, then Deacon would cry and then it would be a total sob fest in here.

Brody sat on the edge of the bed and pulled me into a hug. "I suspected something that first day, remember?" I nodded. "Matt said you were being followed. Yeah, sure it turned out to be Bethany and not that freak stalking you, but you weren't acting right. I should have made you tell me. I should have tickled it out of you and made you move back to the house," he teased.

"God, no." I hugged him back. "I honestly thought I would be okay. He was an annoying creep. He never got close to me or acted threatening until tonight. Yeah, he scared me, but it was more because I didn't know what he would do, rather than because of something he had already done to me."

"Makes sense. Does it hurt?" Spencer gestured to my cheek. "Do you need anything? Say the word and I'll do it."

"It stings a bit, but Dr. Weaver said it will be fine and I won't have a scar."

Trent sat on my other side and swept my hair over my shoulder. "Good, you're too gorgeous for a scar." My dad and brothers had always known about Trent and me and our fake marriage, and they all loved him.

"Let's get you downstairs." The nurse who brought me up here was back with a wheelchair.

"Can I walk?"

She shook her head no. "This is our policy. You had a rough night. Don't be surprised if everything hits you later."

I sat in the chair, and we formed a sad, quiet little parade down the hospital halls until we reached the exit doors where Cade had his SUV waiting.

"Any news? Did they catch him yet?" my dad asked.

"Not yet. But Trevor is the best, so try not to worry."

"Do you want us to come with you, Charlotte? We'll follow along if you want us to," my dad offered.

"No. I love you guys. Go home and get some sleep. I'll be fine, I swear." After hugging them all, Cade helped me into his vehicle, and we headed off to his place.

The drive was silent but not uncomfortable. He held my hand the whole way.

After arriving at his place, he'd carried me into the

house, and now I was in his bedroom—the room we used to share—trying to fall asleep. This wasn't the same bed I used to sleep in with Cade, but it felt like it. This room held some of the best memories of my life and as I sat here, I found myself wishing I had never left.

My life would have been so much simpler and easy instead of this wretched and dangerous mess I had stumbled into over the last few months.

I was in one of Cade's Sweetbriar PD T-shirts, sitting up against the headboard with my knees to my chest wondering how in the heck I would get out of this and why, if I was this exhausted, I couldn't seem fall asleep.

Cade was determined to crash on the couch tonight. He was all about no pressure and no expectations, he was sorry for walking out on me at Vi's book club and blah blah blah. But I didn't care about any of that. I didn't want to be alone. There was no news about my stalker, and I was still pretty scared. Every sound outside made me jump. And since this property backed up to the forest, there were a lot of sounds out there. Animals didn't give a crap about bedtime.

"Damn it," I mumbled as I climbed back under the covers. I was bone tired, my eyes burned and my entire face ached. I needed to go to sleep so bad, but I knew it wasn't going to happen. I tossed to my side, fluffing the pillow beneath my head with a curse. I could never fall asleep on this side, but I wasn't supposed to lie on my stitched-up cheek.

The room was quiet, but my thoughts were loud and

intrusive. Winthrop had been in my garage, listening and watching me for who knows how long.

Cade and I had made love together on the stairs, but we hadn't been alone. Winthrop had heard everything, every private detail. Tears filled my eyes. He had ruined something that was special to me, and it made me sick. Suddenly nauseous, I got up and rushed to the bathroom to throw up.

Footsteps ran up behind me. "Charli, are you okay?" Cade bent and held my hair back. "What's happening? Tell me what's going on."

When I finished, he passed me a tissue. I wiped my mouth and sat with my back against the tub. "He heard us. I didn't tell you before because I didn't think of it until now. He was listening while we were together on the stairs at my place. I can't stand the thought of it—"

"God, Charlotte. I don't know what to say." He looked as disturbed as I felt as he sat cross legged on the floor in front of me. "He's a sick person."

"I can't get it out of my mind. He—he violated us, Cade. He intruded on our intimacy, and I can't stop thinking about it. Help me get it out of my mind."

"It was a definite violation, there's no way around that. But he can't take away how we felt in that moment when we were finally back together. It was beautiful, Charlotte, and it meant everything to me." His face was adamant. "He has nothing to do with how it feels when we're together, how right, and magical it is when we make love. He can't take anything from us unless we allow him to do it. He's nothing, Charlotte, just a sick little man who's going to jail for a long time."

I nodded. I wanted to believe him. I wanted to feel the same way he did. "I'll try to see it like you do."

"I know it's easier said than done. And with all of that being said, the department always recommends therapy for things like this, and I think it's a good idea that we both go."

"I agree. I don't want this coming back to haunt us someday. But mostly, I really don't want to be alone tonight. Go to sleep with me? Please?"

"Of course. I didn't want to—"

"Make me uncomfortable, I know. But I want you with me. Unless you don't feel right about sharing a bed with me after everything—"

"I would love nothing more in the world, Charlotte. It's what I've always wanted. Let's go." He stood and reached for my hands to help me up.

Cade waited in bed for me while I washed my face and tried to convince myself I'd be okay.

Once I'd joined him in bed, he covered us in his blankets and wrapped me in his arms. "I've got you. You're safe to fall asleep."

I shivered in his arms. "Please don't leave me alone. I know it's not fair of me to ask after all the confusion with Trent and the secrets I kept from you."

"None of that matters anymore. I'll stay right here until you wake up, I swear it. You could ask anything of me, and I'll do it. Please believe that."

"Cade—"

"Yeah, baby?"

"Why are you so good to me when—"

"Just let me take care of you. We can talk about—we can talk later, about everything. Tell me anything you want when you're feeling safe again and I'll listen to all of it, I promise. Part of this is my fault. You tried to tell me about Trent several times, and I never wanted to hear it."

"Okay," I murmured into the darkness. "We can talk in the morning."

"Okay." He pulled me close, resting his chin on the top of my head while being careful of my injured cheek.

"I don't know why I ever left you," I whispered. "I should have stayed here in Sweetbriar. Look at what happened—"

"No, don't talk like that." He placed a gentle fingertip to my lips. "You did what you needed to do. You had to go. There were things you needed that I couldn't possibly have given you, and that's okay. I couldn't see then what I see now and I'm sorry—so, so sorry—that I put you in the position to have to choose."

Tears filled my eyes, he brushed them away as they fell. "God, Cade. We've been divorced for so long, but sometimes it still hurts like it was yesterday."

"It hurts me too. I was wrong to let you go without trying to understand you better. I was selfish back then. I had this grandiose idea that I should have been enough for you. That if I loved you enough, I could make you happy here, with me. But I know better now. I've grown up, Charlotte. And I'm not trying to be condescending so please don't take it that way, but I am so fucking proud of you. You did the right thing by going to New York. Look at what you've become."

"Look at you. Your dream has almost come true too. You're going to be the chief, just like you always wanted."

"The more time I spend with you, the more I think *you're* my dream, Charli."

My heart soared at his words. "I feel the same way about you. Being here with you again is magic, it's everything." I paused. "But this is not a second chance, not really. We both know we never had a real shot the first time around because we were just too young. This is us starting over. I think we finally want the same things from our lives."

"What do you want? Tell me. I need to hear it."

I pulled him closer with his shirt clutched in my fists. "You. Only you."

"You have me. You've always had me, Charlotte. I tried to convince myself I was over you so many times, but it was a lie. I never got over you and I never will. You are part of my heart, burned into my soul. What I feel for you is forever."

I nodded, desperate to make him understand how I had always felt. "I swear, the more time we spent apart, the deeper I fell in love with you. I know it doesn't make sense, but it's how I feel—"

"It does make sense, I get it. We're both old enough and smart enough to know what we were missing from our lives. We had to grow up to fully understand what we lost."

"I love how you've always understood me. You're the only one who ever has."

"I'll never let you go again. You know that, right?" He kissed me softly.

"Well, that's good because you're stuck with me."

"This is our path, Charlotte. It's not the one we thought we started on after we walked down the aisle all those years ago, but it belongs to us."

"We're going to be okay. Tell me it's true."

"We're going to be perfect." He kissed me again, slanting his mouth over mine, thrusting his tongue inside with a low groan as his hands slid down my back to grip my hips and drag me closer. "I need you, Charlotte. Is this okay?"

"I don't want you to stop. Make me forget everything but you, Cade. I want it to be only me and you for the rest of the night, and nothing else."

He hooked his thumbs in my waistband and tugged my panties down while I lifted my shirt and slipped out of it. I wanted his skin on mine. I wanted him to erase this entire night from my mind.

He kissed me again, sweet and slow. "I'm going to take care of you. Tell me what you need and it's yours."

"All I need is you," I murmured as I eased into his arms, letting him take the lead. Cade and I had always been fiery, full of passion whenever we were together. But tonight was different. He was tender and soft, as though I would break apart if he wasn't careful.

"Lie back," he whispered as he brushed a kiss against my cheek, over the bandage. "Try to relax, I've got you.

I've been waiting for this, for you to finally be mine again, to stay. You have no idea how much I've missed you all these years, but I'm going to show you right now."

My hands went to his shoulders, tugging his shirt up. "Get this off. I need to feel you."

He shifted up to his knees and with a reach behind the back of his neck, pulled the shirt over his head. "Whenever we're together, it feels like what love is supposed to be. I know that now. With you, I'm needed, I'm wanted, I'm not alone. Promise to let me protect you. Swear it to me, Charli. I can't be without you. Tell me you're mine again. Let me keep you safe."

"You'll never be alone, never again," I promised as I reached for him. "I'm yours—"

"Good girl. God, how I want you." We both gasped as he lowered himself, caging me in with his arms as he entered me. Our eyes met and held as he slid deep.

"You feel so good, Cade." I moaned as he placed kisses along the line of my jaw up to my forehead. "This is how it's supposed to be."

"There's no going back now." His voice was rough like gravel as he buried his face in my neck and thrust gently into me. "I need you too much to ever lose you."

"I need you too, Cade. Please don't stop." I wrapped my legs around his waist to draw him closer.

"I love being inside you, Charli Barrett. There's no better feeling in the world." His voice was a deep groan in my ear.

I slid my hands up his back and around his neck to cup his cheeks in my palms, urging him to move back so I could see his face. "Say that again." His gaze was possessive, the intensity in his eyes lit me on fire. "Please."

"Charli Barrett," he repeated with a dark, sexy grin.

"Yes." I beamed up at him. "God, Cade. I love the sound of that." He kissed me deep. My heart raced in my chest and my toes curled as goosebumps rose over my skin and tingles shot between my legs.

I felt him smile against my lips. "There is nowhere I'd rather be than buried deep inside of this beautiful body," he growled before kissing me again.

I was gone for him. Lost in this perfect moment of clarity and pleasure where he was mine and I was his, and I never wanted it to end. "Make me come. I'm almost there." I threw my arms above my head and arched my back, giving myself over to him like I knew he wanted.

We were fluid, connected, moving as one as he rocked into me. We were finally in a place where the overwhelming feelings we had always carried for each other fit into our lives the way they were meant to.

He reached between our bodies to circle my clit with his thumb, and I writhed beneath him as he drove into me with hard, relentless strokes. I cried out after each one, begging him not to stop.

"Charlotte, I'm close." His thumb moved faster while his other hand slid beneath me to hold my shoulder, keeping me still so he could take me harder and harder until we went off together like fireworks, in bright, bursting, glorious sparks of light.

"Stay right here with me for a minute. Don't go," I whispered.

Bracing himself on his arms, he smoothed my hair back and dropped a kiss to my forehead. He was so beautiful above me in the moonlight and I wanted to memorize the expression he wore so I could keep it like a snapshot in the back of my mind. In his eyes I could see the man I had married long ago, but also so much more. Deep within was the man he had become. He was braver, stronger, fiercely protective and he loved me. I could feel it and I hoped he would say it soon. He was mine again and the world finally made sense. There were no doubts left. We were back, and I would never leave.

"It's okay to go to sleep, baby. You're safe now." He slid out and rolled to his side, gathering me close and holding me tight.

"Goodnight," I murmured. My eyelids grew heavy. I smiled as I drifted off in his arms.

"I love you Charlotte," he whispered. "I always have."

I woke up to sunlight warming my face as it filtered through the sheer curtains covering the sliding glass door.

Cade was sitting in the chair by the bed reading a book—my latest book, the Jaden Skerrit introductory book. I yawned through my smile.

"There she is." His voice was gentle, and his return smile was like nothing I'd ever seen cross his face. It was tender, almost reverent. "Good morning, baby."

"Good morning. Did you sleep? Is everything okay?"

He set the book aside. "No, I didn't sleep. I wanted to be awake in case you had a bad dream, or you needed me."

My heart swelled. It wasn't big enough to hold all the love that had surged into it.

"Cade." I held up my arms as tears filled my eyes. "Thank you. You made me okay. You kept me safe. You helped me sleep. I—" Tears filled my eyes and I looked away.

"Hey, you don't need to thank me." He pulled me into his arms after joining me in bed. "I'll always be here for you. Count on it."

"I do, I will count on it from now on. And I'm here for you too, Cade."

He stroked his hand over my hair. "Are you up for the day? Do you need more rest?"

"I'm up. Is there any news?" I rested my head against his chest, enjoying the warmth of his skin.

He sighed and pulled my even closer. "They haven't caught him. But we now know that he stole his brother's identity when he came here. They look almost identical, so it was easy for him to use his identification. The man Trent saw get on the plane was Howard. Douglas has always been the one stalking you, and Howard had no idea about anything that had been going on with you, the arrests, or the restraining order. Obviously, they aren't close. According to Howard, Douglas has always been prone to obsessive and violent behaviors and has been in and out of therapy and prison for years. He's a psychopath, Charlotte. He has warrants for his arrest in several states and yours isn't the only restraining order he's had, it's just the most recent. He shouldn't be out. But it is what it is."

I shivered. It all gave me the willies. "That all fits, I guess. I mean, it's sad. He should be locked up somewhere instead of running around harassing me, or anyone else, for that matter."

"Yeah, it's pretty terrible. There was no way their parents or Howard could force him to get help or stay in treatment. From what Trevor said, they washed their hands of him. There was nothing they could do."

"Damn."

"Enough about that. Trevor will catch him. How are you feeling?"

I shrugged, my shoulders rubbing against his solid chest. "My face hurts. My body aches. I'm still tired, but it will take at least a week of uninterrupted sleep to fix that."

"My poor Charli." He dropped a kiss to the top of my head. "Would you like me to run you a hot bath? I'll fix breakfast and make coffee while you're in there."

"I have to say this. There are good men in this world —my dad and brothers are proof of that. But you are on another level."

"Don't make me blush." He chuckled.

"Oh my god, do it. Please blush. It will only make you hotter," I teased as I kissed his bare chest, then traced the tattoo of my name with a fingertip.

Chapter 23
Cade

I stood up to go run her bath, stopping once I made it to the bathroom door to turn back and look at her. She was beautiful in my bed, with her hair a mess and her sleepy blue eyes. It felt like I had been transported to the past, or maybe lost in one of the dreams I used to have right after she left town. I would wake up alone, haunted by her face and desperate to be with her again.

"I can't believe this is real," she whispered as if she had been reading my mind.

The sound of her voice pulled me back into reality and I smiled. "It's real. Never doubt how I feel about you."

"I won't, even though you may be too good to be true. Do you have an extra toothbrush I could use? I'm going to kiss the heck out of you when I get out of the tub."

"Of course." I smiled sheepishly. "Everything you'll need is in the same place you put it when we first moved in—towels, extra toothbrushes, soap. It's all new, of course, but yeah, I'll admit your organizational skills can't be beat."

She giggled. "This is like coming back home." She froze. "Um, I didn't mean that. Is it too soon to mean that? *Ugh!* I'm sorry, forget what I just said—"

"I want you to mean that, because I mean what I'm about to say. This has always been your home and it always will be. No woman but you has ever been in here."

"Oh, Cade . . ."

I looked away. It still made me nervous to be so vulnerable. "So, now that we've moved beyond you being mine only in Sweetbriar, you're going to let me take care of you like I need to do."

"Okaaaaaay . . . But what does that even mean?"

"Things changed between us last night and since we're officially together again everywhere, I'm going to cross all kinds of boundaries. You're not going back to that townhouse—ever. One, they haven't found Winthrop yet, and two, that place is terrible. You need a garage to park in and someone to take care of your porch when it gets mossy. You need someone who shovels snow and is willing to start your car and warm it up for you when it's cold outside."

"And that someone is you?"

"Damn straight."

Her eyes sparkled as she smiled at me. "Then I have a few requests too."

I leaned back against the bathroom door frame and

grinned at her. "Give it to me. I want to hear all of it. I'm listening."

She sat up. "Tell me exactly what you want from me. Stop being sweet and giving and understanding and supportive of my dreams, damn it. Demand that I stay with you. I can write here. I did what I needed to do in New York—that's over and done. I'd much rather write with your mom at Violet's, or out on the deck."

"Move back to Sweetbriar, Charlotte. I'm begging you."

"Consider it done." She slapped the mattress for emphasis, and I laughed.

"Your turn. That was pretty much all of my wants." The smile wouldn't leave my face; I was about to burst with happiness. "Tell me what you want, Charli."

She stood and crossed the room to cup my face and smack a fast kiss to my lips. "I want to burn your dinner again and give you blow jobs in the bathtub like young Charlotte used to do. I want us to get married, and it's gonna be big and fancy this time, with everyone there. There will be no sneaking off to elope, no Vegas, no Elvis, no jeans and T-shirts, and no honeymoon in a cheap motel. I want it to be huge, Cade. I want us to adopt a dog together, or maybe a cat, and I want to live right here in this house and have babies with you someday. But the bottom line is, I just want you, Caden Andrew Barrett. In my life. Every day. Every night. All the time. Please tell me you want that too because I love you, I always have, and I always will. This is forever."

"I love you too, Charlotte. I want you to stay with me and never leave. I know now that it's all I ever wanted."

"You got it, Cade. All of me—my heart, my soul, my body, my screwy brain. But most of all, you have my love." She winked at me and held a hand up. "We're not kissing again until I brush my teeth and take that bath. I'm grody. Like, I can taste my breath. I apologize if I grossed you out when I kissed you before."

I burst out laughing. "No way. Not possible. I even love your not-quite-as-bad-as-you-think-it-is morning breath." I laid one on her to prove it. "Coffee and breakfast will be waiting when you get out of the tub. I washed your pajamas while you were sleeping, but I couldn't find your panties. I don't know where they landed when I threw them last night, and I didn't want to turn the light on and risk waking you up. You'll have to go commando until we can pick up some of your things."

"Don't worry about it. I won't need the panties because you're going to let me do all the naked things I want to you after we have breakfast. I haven't been on top yet and I've been looking forward to a good ride. Then after we blow each other's minds, we'll take a long nap. I have our day all planned out in my mind."

"I don't know how I ever lived without you." I cupped her cheek, amazed that I got so lucky to have her back in my life. And also worried because I knew all the jokes and flirting were covering up her fear and exhaustion.

"You'll never have to live without me, ever again."

"I love you, Charlotte. So much."

"I love you too, Cade. We're forever this time."

* * *

We had finished breakfast. Our coffee mugs and dishes were on the table, and she was standing in front of me, nestled in my arms, as we looked over the mountains and started to settle into our future together. I had it all back and I was ready for more, but there was no need to rush. We had time—all the time in the world.

"I want you to know something," I murmured, my voice ruffling her soft hair along with the breeze.

"Tell me," she whispered.

"When we were young, I loved you the best I knew how. I thought it would be enough, but it wasn't. I just realized it couldn't have been enough back then because this finally is. I love all of you now, Charlotte, and I wouldn't change a thing. I love your ambition, I love your goals, and your drive to be more. I even love that you left me to take what you needed out of life, because now you're back and you're amazing."

"I love you too, Cade. More than I ever knew was possible."

"We're going to get it right this time, I know it." I pulled her tight against me, the soft curves of her body molded to mine, and I sighed. We were both all in this time. Nothing could come between us ever again.

She turned in my arms to look up at me. "My heart is in the palm of your hand again, Cade," she whispered. "Please keep it safe."

"Always," I vowed, lifting her face to mine for a kiss.

After she left for New York, I'd played it safe. I shut down and never reopened my heart for someone else to hurt me. Hell, I'd even shut Charlotte out when we started up again with all the conditions I had set and my refusal to listen to her. I realized I'd been playing it scared, not safe. I vowed to never close myself off again. Charlotte deserved all of me, and I deserved to have love in my life again.

"Let's go back to bed," she murmured against my lips. "But sadly, I might be too tired to be on top. We can do that tomorrow."

I tucked a lock of hair behind her ear. "You can be on top whenever you want. We have nothing but time."

"Oh wait, you were up all night. I can rally. Let's have more coffee first. Or we can both go to sleep for a while?"

"How about you take a nap and I'll sit with you while you sleep. We're not leaving this house until—"

"Until they catch him," she finished.

I nodded. "Exactly. I haven't heard from Trevor in about an hour. I'm starting to think—" I was interrupted by the sound of both our cell phones ringing.

The number on mine was unknown. "Cade Barrett here," I answered.

"I'm going to grab my phone real quick, it's on the deck," she mouthed, pointing to the door.

I nodded as she crossed the living room and slid the door open.

Whoever was on the line was mumbling so bad I

couldn't make it out. "Who is this? I can't hear you. No, my name is not Jaden."

Jaden.

Dread ran through my body as my eyes shot toward Charlotte outside. She blew me kiss and waved. I let out a relieved sigh as I waved back. "You have the wrong number—"

"Cade!"

Her piercing scream sent my heart plummeting as I dropped my phone and raced to the deck.

Chapter 24
Charlotte

My cell stopped ringing. "Dang it." I picked it up to see who I had missed.

"Adaline." I felt a hand wind up in my hair at the same time his creepy as hell voice filled my ears.

"Let me go!" I gasped, struggling to break free. "Cade!" I managed to scream before his other hand slipped over my mouth. My eyes watered as he tightened his grip in my hair and twisted the strands. I bit down on his hand, and he yanked my head back with a vicious pull as he dragged me toward the stairs that led off the deck.

"Damn it, let me go!" I kicked back into his shin and stomped on his foot. I wasn't letting this freak get me off the deck. No way.

Cade's massive deck had stairs that led down to a small grassy back yard, but there was no fence separating it from the forest that lie beyond, and the nearest neighbors were at least half a mile away. We were mountain rural up here and almost completely isolated.

I knew my life depended on me staying on this deck.

"Adaline! Stop fighting me!" He hit me in the side with the closed fist of the hand I'd bitten, and I flinched. It hurt. He rained blows over the side of my face and my upper chest, and I gagged when his fist connected with my neck.

"Stop it!" I reached back and grabbed between his legs to squeeze with everything I had in me, then blindly punched backward until he squealed and hunched over. Unfortunately, I couldn't get loose from that hand in my hair. But I managed to twist around and get a good look at all the crazy up close. His eyes were wide and vacant; it was like looking into a black hole.

I kicked out, but his hand in my hair had me off-balance and we fell to the ground. We struggled briefly before he pinned me to the ground and held me with one arm around my throat and that damn hand in my hair. I tried to send an elbow into his ribs, but his arm flexed around my neck, and I struggled to breathe. "Hold still and I'll stop choking you." I froze. Every single thing I'd learned in Krav Maga went out the window as I gasped for breath. Finally, he lessened the pressure on my throat and I could breathe.

What felt like forever but was only seconds later, Cade's footsteps pounded over the deck as he rushed toward us while dogs started barking in the distance. *What the hell? Dogs?*

"Let her go!" Cade yelled through his clenched jaw. I

could see him try to figure out how to help me get away without getting my hair ripped from my scalp or the breath squeezed from my lungs. "That's my wife you're manhandling and you're not going anywhere."

"Freeze, Winthrop!" It was Trevor. I almost cried with relief when I saw him coming up the deck stairs, gun drawn, with Quinn following close behind. "You're surrounded, and you're under arrest. Let her go."

Winthrop couldn't get around them and there was no other way off the deck.

"I can't. She has to fix our story first." He jerked me around with his hand in my hair, so we rolled into a weird half-sitting position. "You have to change it, Adaline! Fix us or I'll have to kill him. Jaden has to go, you know that. You know it because I warned you SO MANY TIMES!" he screamed, tightening his arm around my neck again.

I could see the fear and rage in Cade's eyes when he growled, "Let her go, Winthrop!"

Winthrop's hand in my hair tightened and I whimpered, frozen in place.

"Trevor, move in. You too, Quinn," Cade ordered. Trevor moved to one side, followed by Quinn on the other, while another officer took his position at the top of the stairs to ensure Winthrop couldn't get off the deck.

I glanced down at the yard and saw other officers moving up the stairs to line the deck. Cade's place was surrounded by police, and a few of them had dogs. They must have been searching in the woods.

Just then, a pickup truck skidded to a stop along the edge of the driveway. Three of my brothers vaulted out of the bed, two with crowbars and one with a baseball bat, just as the doors flew open and my other two brothers and dad jumped out of the cab. I could hear their yelling as officers from the yard ran over to keep them back.

Winthrop used the momentary distraction to stumble to his feet clumsily, dragging me up with him. He pulled my head against his chest then placed his chin against my neck. There was no way anyone could help me get away without risking him ripping the hair out of my head, and no clear shot that didn't put me at risk. We were too close together.

Plus, I didn't want him to die. I just wanted him to let go of me and leave me the hell alone.

"Let me go," I begged. "I'll fix it. I'll write whatever you want me to if you let go." My eyes watered from the pain in my scalp.

"I don't believe you." He sounded desperate, which scared me. "How am I supposed to believe you, Adaline? I can't trust you anymore, not with him here, not with how he feels about you. I took the note he left you. I know he wants you back. I know everything. Tell him to leave. Tell him you want me, not him!"

"I want you, of course I do. I promise I'll write what you want. I swear it." *Note? I knew that short note was off!*

"Liar. Liar. Liar. Liar!" he chanted as tightened his grip on my hair and around my neck.

"Oh, god. Please let me go," I gasped, flinching at the vice grip he had on me.

"Quinn, go inside and get scissors from the house,

kitchen drawer by the fridge." Cade barked. "Just in case I have to cut some of her hair free." *Could he rip my scalp off this way?*

Winthrop pulled even harder on my hair, and I cried out.

Cade swooped in then, performing a move that would have made my Krav Maga instructor proud. In one motion, he slipped a hand under Winthrop's arm, breaking me free of his chokehold, and twisting Winthrop against the deck railing in some kind of hold so tight he couldn't move.

His firm grip in my hair meant the motion had me stumbling along with them, but fortunately, Trevor swooped in at the same moment, his hands pressed to the top of my head down over Winthrop's to prevent anymore pulling. Winthrop still had me pulled tight to his chest, but the relief was immediate despite the still-throbbing pain. Could hair follicles get bruised? I could feel him trying to pry loose Winthrop's grip, but every movement made me flinch.

"You're not getting off this deck, Winthrop," Cade growled. "I will not leave, and I will not let you go. There is no way in hell I'm giving you another chance to hurt her."

"You don't belong here!" Winthrop shrieked back. "You don't belong here with her. Not like I do. I'm her Tim. We're married!"

Winthrop screamed in frustration against the side of my face when he tried to move his body and couldn't. My ears rang and my head pounded from the echo of his shrill voice in my head. Between that and the searing pain in my scalp, I was in real danger of fainting.

"I don't feel so great. I think I'm going to pass out," I informed them.

"Go ahead, baby. Catch her, Matt. Hold her up."

My eyelids fluttered as Trevor continued trying to work my hair free, and Matt stood in front of me, holding my in a quasi-hug, helping me stay on my feet. "Oh, hey, Matt. How did you get back here?"

"I went through the house," he grunted.

"Don't let them cut off my hair," I whispered loudly. I knew I wasn't making sense anymore, but it was either space out or freak out. Somehow, spacing out felt productive and possibly even helpful, so I went with it.

The sounds of Winthrop trying to break free of Cade's grip swirled around me. "Adaline!" he yelled. "Adaline, you're mine!" Suddenly, I felt very woozy.

"Don't cut her hair," Matt said.

"Thank you for your support. I think I might pass out soon. My legs are shaking."

"No problem, babe, I got you. I won't let you fall. Just take a deep breath."

"'Kay . . ." I inhaled a huge breath. It helped a little bit.

I could feel Trevor trying to pull strands of my hair free when Hunter hollered from below, "Choke him out, Cade!"

"Just shoot him!" Spencer bellowed. "He'll let her go if he's bleeding too much to stand up."

Cade, who was doing his best to keep Winthrop still

while Trevor worked on my hair, barked out, "Not necessary!"

"Who cares if it's necessary?" Brody yelled. "Just get her free before he hurts her any worse."

I could feel Winthrop still struggling through his grip in my hair. Trevor's efforts made sure it no longer hurt, but he was not letting go. *When will this ever end?*

"I'll punch him in the face!" Tucker offered. "Police can't punch people, but I'm happy to."

"You can't punch him in the face, dumbass." Hunter bit out. "You might hit Charlotte instead. He's too close to her."

"Shut up!" my father yelled from the stairs. I hadn't seen him climb them, but I was sure glad he had. "They have it under control. They don't need help from you knuckleheads."

Seeing my dad made my eyes well up. "Daddy . . ." I choked on the lump on my throat as tears spilled down my cheeks.

His tone was soothing when he responded, "I'm here, sweetheart. You're going to be just fine. Hold on." He gave me an encouraging smile.

"Okay." I took another deep breath. I could feel Winthrop's grip on my hair lessening as Trevor continued to work it free.

"I almost got it, Charlotte," Trevor told me. "You're doing great."

"You're hurting my hand! You're going to break my fingers!" Winthrop yelled at Trevor, but the full force of his voice went straight in my ear.

That was it. I'd hit my limit. "Your fingers?" I was no longer scared; I was infuriated. "Who cares about your fucking fingers! Shut your fucking mouth!" Between that sweaty hand in my hair, his hairy arm around my neck, his hot, smelly breath all over the side of my face, and all the yelling, I'd had enough. "Let me go, you unbearable prick!"

"You're mine, Adaline!" he shrieked.

"Oh yeah? Then let me give you this!" I flipped from freeze to fight and slammed my elbow into his ribs as hard as I could. He grunted and his grip loosened just enough that Trevor was able to free the last strands of my hair. He had Winthrop's arm bent and twisted into a hold immediately.

Matt pulled me clear as my dad rushed forward and gasped out, "Thank god!" He turned me into my dad's waiting arms with a smile.

"Thanks, Matt."

"Of course, Charlotte." He ducked his head and looked me in the eye. "Make sure you talk to someone when this hits you. Okay?"

I nodded. My body felt like it was deflating. I held tight to my dad as my adrenaline levels crashed and my knees went weak. The deck was spinning, and my vision was turning white at the edges.

I watched as Trevor handcuffed Winthrop and read him his rights.

Winthrop screamed, "Adaline! Help me!" as he was escorted in the direction of the stairs.

I tucked my face into my dad's chest and held on as my brain started to come back online.

"You're going to be okay, my brave Charlotte. I'll make sure of it. We all will." My father soothed me by patting my back and stroked my hair gently, easing the ache from all the pulling.

"Give me five minutes alone with that jackass before you take him to jail." Spencer demanded. I lifted my head to see all my brothers had pushed their way up the stairs onto the deck and were crowded behind my father. "That's all I'll need to teach him a lesson."

"I'm the oldest," Hunter protested. "I should get the five minutes."

"How about we each get one minute." Brody, ever the peacemaker, suggested. "He can learn five different lessons that way."

I scoffed. "I'm sorry, but if anyone gets five minutes, it's going to be me. I'm the one he's been harassing all these months. And, hell, this is for sure going to come back to haunt me. Call that therapist, Cade. I need a freaking appointment. As soon as possible."

"Charli baby. Come here, I need to hold you." I turned to find Cade reaching for me. My father let me go and with all the relief in the world, I slid into Cade's waiting embrace.

His warm arms wrapped around me, cocooning me in safety. "Oh god, Cade. Please tell me this is over."

"It's over. Between what he did to you and the other outstanding warrants, he's going away for a long time."

Chapter 25
Cade

Two Weeks Later

I watched from the doorway as she shifted side to side, studying her reflection in the mirror on the back of the bathroom door. She has never truly realized how stunning she is. Her lips pursed as she applied her lipstick. She took a step back, scanned her reflection one more time, then flipped her hair over her shoulder with a sigh.

"Hey, gorgeous." She jumped, squealing as she spun around.

"You scared the heck out of me, Cade!"

"I'm sorry. I didn't mean to startle you. Quit worrying, you're perfect."

Her smile was soft as she thanked me. "Well, you make me feel perfect. You look handsome tonight."

"I merely state the obvious and thank you. Are you ready for this? It's your first official Barrett Sunday dinner since we got back together." She was beautiful in a dress the color of her eyes and high heeled shoes that made it easier for me to bend down to kiss her. So I did. With a hand at the back of her neck, I pulled her in. I would never get tired of the feel of her lips against mine.

Her twinkling eyes met mine after we stepped apart. "I'm so ready for this. I can't wait. I can't believe Dahlia agreed to one big party instead of throwing one for each bit of good news. This goes against all her beliefs as wife, mother, and extrovert. The real question is, are you ready?"

"Are you kidding? All my dreams have come true after all. I'm one hundred percent ready."

Tonight wasn't an ordinary Barrett Sunday dinner. My father had retired, and I was the new chief of the Sweetbriar Police Department. Charlotte and I were official, and tonight we would celebrate all of it over my mother's filet of beef and truffled mashed potatoes.

"Well, we still need to get a dog. So not *every* dream . . ." She ran her hands up my chest then flung her arms around my neck.

"We'll go to the shelter tomorrow." I kissed her forehead, then her still-bandaged cheek.

"Kiss me for real again. I need more before we go." Her mouth curved into a pouty smile.

"Could be dangerous. We have to be at my parent's house in a half hour."

"We have time."

"We have all the time in the world. But you know how my mother gets when anyone is late. And you know how I get once you get me started . . ."

"Aww. Okay." She smoothed the wrinkles she'd made on my shirt from clutching it in her fists. "You're probably right." Her eyes shifted up to mine through her lashes and I groaned as her hand drifted lower and her smile got bigger.

"You're making it hard to say no, Charli. In more ways than one." I backed her up against the wall and ground myself against her. "And for the record. I want you. Right here. Right now."

"Who says you can't have me?" She spun to the side and placed her hands on the dresser. "You're the boss of you," she said over her shoulder. "And if you're a good boy, I'll let you be the boss of me for a few minutes, too."

She was too sexy to resist. She had been insatiable ever since that day with Winthrop on the deck. Like she was using sex to escape the memories. As long as we continued to work it through with the therapist, I figured it was fine. And we had always run hot, so I wasn't complaining.

"Lift up your dress." My hands went to my belt to undo it. I was already painfully hard for her, a state she obviously took pride in keeping me in. And saying no when she needed me was the last thing I ever wanted to do.

"God, yes." She pushed her panties down and did what I said.

I gripped her curvy hips and thrust into her. "Are you always gonna be ready for me like this?"

"Probably." She panted as she widened her stance. "You drive me crazy."

"Touch yourself."

"Ahhh," she moaned. I felt her fingers moving between us, stroking both me and herself as I made love to her in long slow drives into her body.

"We have to hurry, baby." I placed my hands on the dresser on either side of her. "Take me, Charlotte. Make yourself come."

She drove herself back on my cock and I braced myself, holding still as she tightened around me in a swirling wave. "I love you." She moaned as one of her hands moved over mine, interlocking and holding tight while the other still circled her clit, driving herself higher until she fell over the edge with a shuddering gasp.

"Stay still for me." I pushed her down over the dresser until her undamaged cheek touched the smooth wooden surface. Her skin was so fucking soft beneath my palms; I couldn't get enough. Part of me was desperate to devour her while the other part wanted to drop to my knees and worship her.

I wrapped an arm around her waist and with the tip of my finger, I teased her clit as I pounded into her. "You're gonna come again, Charlotte. Be a good girl and give it to me fast so I can let go with you," I grunted. "Hurry." With my other hand, I pinched her nipple through the silk of her dress and worked it with my fingers.

"God, Cade, what is happening?"

I groaned at the feel of the little squeezing pulses, the rolling sway of her hips. Her back arched for me, and her palms slapped the dresser as she cried out.

"Me and you is what's happening. Hurry, baby."

"Keep going," she begged. "Don't stop."

I fucked her hard until we both exploded, coming together until we were both gasping for breath and spent from our orgasms.

"I love you too. More than the entire world." I whispered into her ear as I hugged her close. "Now we need to get going."

"I need to go clean up first—"

"Oh no you're not." I sucked on the nape of her neck, hard enough to leave a slight mark, and she shivered. "You're keeping me inside until we get home, so all night long you'll remember what I just did to you." I slid my hand up her thigh and pushed my fingers inside of her. "Get those panties back on."

I let her up and she turned in my arms to face me. She bit her lip as her eyes sparked into mine. "I love you like this," she confessed.

My lips quirked up at the corner. "I know you do."

* * *

I drove up the winding driveway to my parent's property with my hand on her leg laying claim. I was tempted to turn around, go back home and get into bed with her. But we couldn't miss dinner tonight. It was too important to our families. Plus, I'd made surprise plans for dessert once dinner was over.

I pulled in next to Rose's car and parked. "Stay there, I'll come around and let you out." I opened the door and grabbed her by the waist, letting her slide down my body as I helped her out.

"Hello, you two." Rose popped open the back of her VW and removed a cooler bag. "I brought the salad. Mom actually let me make something. Sure, it didn't *technically* involve cooking but I'm totally counting it. Help me out, Cade. Trevor is already inside with the kids. I'm meeting them here." I grabbed one of the bags from the back.

"Relatable." Charlotte laughed. "My family won't let me cook anything either."

"You set one kitchen fire too many times and people freak out. Am I right?" Rose laughed.

"Exactly. I deserve a second chance, and maybe some cooking lessons."

"Lucky you're with Cade. He's on his way to expert level cook status."

They chatted all the way up the walkway while I took it all in. The front of the house had been decorated with a "Congratulations" banner for me and my father and there were balloons and streamers everywhere.

"Hello!" My mother called from the porch. "We're all out back. It's such a nice day I figured we would have dinner on the patio."

"Hey, Dahlia." My mother kissed Charlotte on both cheeks and hugged her.

"I'm so glad you're okay, sweetheart. Come inside and let me pour you a glass of wine."

She looked back at me, and I smiled. "Go for it. I need to talk to my dad."

Rose took the second cooler bag from me and followed Mom and Charlotte into the dining room.

I found my father on the couch in the living room. He was still and quiet, sitting there with a beer in his hand.

"Hey," I greeted.

"Cade. Sit with me."

I joined him, sitting on the chair adjacent to the couch. "How are you feeling? I'm nervous as fuck."

"Same. I worked my whole life to be what I was, and now it's finished. I feel a bit adrift. But also, I'm ready to start a new chapter. Sleeping in sounds good too."

"I think I feel something similar. Not the adrift part, but definitely ready to start a new chapter."

"I'm happy for you, son. You're finally on the path you wanted to follow."

"Yeah, I am. I shouldn't have been so stubborn all these years. I could have had her back a long time ago."

"Regret is pointless. And you don't know that. You could have pursued her years ago and it might not have worked out like it did now. I'm a big believer in things falling into place when they're meant to. Something pulled you back together this time."

"It was Winthrop. She was being stalked." I huffed a laugh. "She was in town longer because of him."

"Nah, that wasn't it." He shook his head and grinned

at me. "Cade, you do realize she spent at least a month in Sweetbriar for Christmas every year?" I shrugged; I hadn't thought of that. "Sometimes she'd be at her dad's place for the entire summer. She was here all the time, for every single one of her brother's birthdays, and for Tucker's kids' birthdays too. It wasn't the stalker. You were both just ready this time around."

"Maybe you're right."

"Of course I'm right. I'm always right. But that's my burden to bear." We both laughed and he sipped his beer. "How's she doing?"

"Better. She had a few nightmares right after it happened. But I think therapy is helping. We go every other day. Next week we'll start with once a week. Plus, she's living with me now. We moved all her stuff in last week, so she doesn't have to worry about sleeping alone."

"And you?"

"I'm fine. I go to therapy with her. I know it's helping both of us. And not just with the Winthrop situation. But our relationship too. We're stronger than ever."

"That's good. So, let's see it."

"See what?"

"The ring."

My eyebrows shot up in surprise. "How did you know?"

"Along with always being right, I know everything." He chuckled. "Okay, fine. Your mother told me." Mom had gone ring shopping with me. I told her I needed something emerald cut and she had done the rest.

"I was gonna say . . ." I stood and pulled the ring box from my pocket, tossing it to him with a grin.

"Pretty. She'll love it. But she'd say yes to you without it. That's another way you know she's your one and only. Don't let her go this time. Charlotte is a wonderful girl—a Barrett for life." He tossed it back to me and I stuffed it in my pocket for later.

Chapter 26
Charlotte

He raised my hand to his lips over the console and kissed the back. "Want to stop at Holloway's for a drink before we go home?"

"Sure, why not? We can sit in our booth and reminisce. Nostalgia doesn't feel bad anymore, not when I have you back in my life."

He turned and winked at me. "I know what you mean. I feel the same way."

"Good. I want to make you happy, Cade."

"You do." He swung into the Holloway's parking lot and found a space up front.

I followed him inside to our spot. Savannah waved to us from behind the bar as we slid into the back corner booth where so many of our memories together had been made.

Our eyes met and he smiled as he reached into his pocket then slid a black velvet ring box onto the table, opening it to reveal an emerald cut engagement ring. It twinkled in the light, and I burst into tears.

I'm not a big crier. But anyone would cry over this.

This man.

This ring.

This perfect moment that I was lucky to share with him twice.

"Oh, you!" I burst into tears. "Cade . . ."

"Stop crying so I can ask you." He chuckled and wiped my tears away with a thumb.

"Can't do it. Ask me anyway. I'm sure I can choke out a yes."

"Charlotte Keli Cassidy-Barrett for life—will you make me the happiest man on the planet and marry me again?"

I opened my mouth, and a huge ass sob came out of it instead of a *yes*. I fluttered my fingers in front of my face and nodded my head while I tried to answer him again. But I had no words. I sputtered out another sob and covered my mouth with my hand.

I, Charlotte Cassidy, an author who wrote words for a damn living, couldn't manage to say the one word that would change my life in all the best ways.

"Baby . . ." He pulled me close and kissed the crown of my head. "I love you so much."

"Yes," I whispered against his broad chest as he held me. "Yes. I love you!"

He pulled back and took my hand, and as my shoulders shook and the tears flowed, he slid the most perfectly gorgeous emerald cut ring on my finger.

And I lost my damn mind, I couldn't see through the tears, I couldn't talk through the lump in my throat. I couldn't even think, I was so happy.

Something had broken inside of me. Like a dam had burst and all the feelings I'd been denying over the years I'd spent without him came flooding out—relief, joy, happiness. But mostly, it was the simple gratitude that I was able to follow my heart home to Sweetbriar and let it lead me back to him.

<h1 style="text-align:center">Chapter 27
Charlotte</h1>

Charlotte Keli Cassidy-Barrett

R ed lips, serious glam. I smiled at myself in the mirror as I tossed my lip brush to the counter. I was channeling Keli Marlowe's look on my wedding day, but I felt one hundred percent like myself.

Charlotte Cassidy, soon to be legally Barrett for life.

"Oh, Charli," Gwen brushed her tears away as she came up behind me. "You're so beautiful."

I turned. "Thank you, Gwen. Look at you, maid of honor. You're stunning."

"Thanks. But more important than how gorgeous we both look today is the fact I have my best friend back for good." She hugged me and I tried not to cry. Even though most of my makeup was waterproof, I still didn't need any tears. Getting all red and blotchy from crying was a real concern with my fair skin and I wanted flawless wedding photos. I was determined to live the entire bridal experience I'd missed out on during our first go-around. The go-around with Trent didn't count, it was a fake courthouse thing that meant nothing. I wanted this to be perfect for Cade and me —something beautiful we would remember forever.

"Can we come in?" Violet popped her head through the partially closed doorway of my suite at the recently renovated Sweetbriar Inn.

"Yes. Oh, my goodness, you're all stunning." While Gwen was my maid of honor, each one of Cade's sisters was a bridesmaid.

My wedding colors were shades of black and silver. Gwen was in a deep black beaded strapless sheath, while Cade's sisters wore matching dresses in shades running from dark gray to a light sparkling silver. They looked like an ombré midnight rainbow.

I had told Cade our second wedding would be big, and I'd meant it. I'd rented out the entire inn. But since Cade's Grandma Rosemary still owned it, she cut me a sweet deal. This place was gorgeous—an old Victorian mansion at the edge of town. After her husband died, she shut the inn down and retired from running it. Holly was currently working on restoring it back to its former glory and she'd moved into one of the suites.

Black and white roses covered nearly every surface. Flameless candles and twinkly lights provided sparkly illumination, and all the guests were dressed in black. But not me; I was in white silk and lace. My hair was in a fabulous French twist and my veil was a work of art. My dress even had a train; when I walked down the aisle, I would be followed by ten feet of beaded lace.

I looked up as Dahlia entered the room along with her sister, Delphine, and mother, Rosemary. "We have something for you."

I turned and beckoned them in with a huge smile. "What is it?"

"You're about to become a Barrett again, but we wanted to give you something from us. Something all us girls have." Cade's sisters circled around me. Tears threatened to spill but I blinked them back.

Dahlia placed a pale pink jewelry bag into my open palm.

"Thank you." After inhaling a deep breath, I opened it. Strung on a delicate platinum chain was a single, perfect pink pearl. I looked up to see that they each had a matching necklace around their necks, and I immediately wanted to wear mine too. "Oh gosh. Help me put this on, Gwen. Please."

Gwen took it from me and fastened it. I'd never had a mother or a sister or an aunt. I grew up with the best dad ever and wonderful brothers and I never lacked love and affection, but standing here right now, I could feel what I had missed out on.

"These came from a necklace Cade's grandpa gave me after we got married," Rosemary explained. "A couple years ago, I decided I wanted all my girls to have a piece of it."

She held her arms up and I hugged her. "Welcome back to the family, Charlotte. We missed you."

"I missed you too. All of you. So much."

I bit the inside of my cheek hard. I was not going to cry. No way.

"Are you ready?" My dad's voice in the hall made us all stand at attention.

"Yes," I replied. This was happening. I beamed at every face in this room. "I am about to burst!" I couldn't help it, I twirled. Then I stumbled over the train and almost went down. But Gwen caught me before I could fall.

"Girl, I warned you about this. Trains are not for the faint of heart. And definitely not for spinning."

"Let's do this," Rose took my hand. "A girl can never have enough sisters. I'm so happy."

"We all are." Violet leaned in and kissed my cheek

"There is no getting away this time," Lily added. "We won't let you."

"I'm here for good," I promised. "I love you all."

I watched as they all made their way to the entrance of the ballroom where Cade waited, then took my father's arm.

"I love you, princess."

"Love you too, Dad."

The music started and my smile grew bigger. For a second, I got worried because my face was in real danger of freezing in a permanent expression of my joy.

As I got ready to marry the man I had loved forever, my eyes were dry, but my heart was full.

Maybe tonight was Cade's turn to cry. Tears filled his eyes when I took my place at the start of the rose petal-covered aisle.

"I love you!" I shouted, making him smile through his tears.

"I love you too, Charli."

We had strayed from the path we began so many years ago, but with each step down this aisle I knew we'd never lose our way again.

This time was forever.

And when my father placed my hand in Cade's, my soul sighed in contentment, knowing it was finally back home where it belonged.

Chapter 28
One Year Later

Book Baby

Charlotte

"Congratulations on your new book baby!" My sister-in-law, Violet squealed as she tugged me into her arms for a hug. "I'm so happy you're here. I'm so happy you're back with Cade and that the two of you are doing so well. It's been a whole year, Charli! New book, new marriage, new life! *GAH!* This book club is going to be epic. So much happiness!"

Little did she know...

My latest Adaline Paige mystery, *My One and Only*, had just hit e-readers and bookshelves today and I was honoring the occasion with a release party at Violet's coffee shop. Since I'd moved back to town and remarried her brother, I had a standing invitation to take over her weekly book club whenever I wanted, and tonight was my night to celebrate.

As usual, she'd gone all out with fancy snacks and drinks. Her shop was decorated with candles and streamers, and my books were distributed in piles across the various tables around the shop for people to buy and have me sign. It was set up to be a great evening.

My bestie, Gwen, passed me one of Vi's signature martinis and held her glass up for a "Cheers!" but I only touched the glass to my mouth with a smile. Not one drop of alcohol would pass these lips, not after the news I got this morning.

"I'll grab some snacks. Save us a spot on the sofa," she called over her shoulder as she headed for the buffet table in the corner.

Elizabeth, my Sweetbriar Stop-and-Go confidant and Gwen's sister, not to mention my biggest reader-fan-supporter in town, shot me a wink. She'd been the one to ring up the ten different varieties of pregnancy tests I had panic tossed across the counter at her along with a plethora of snacks and candy earlier today. In fact, she'd been the one to suggest the huge bottle of water I would require in order to produce enough pee to take all the tests. Elizabeth had always been a helper.

Those ten minutes in the Stop-and-Go restroom had been the most highly charged of my life. Waiting for all the lines to turn pink or blue, the tiny little plus signs to form, and the word *"pregnant"* to cover the little gray screens had been an experience I would never forget as long as I lived. I'd ran out of the store with my plastic bag full of positive tests like I was escaping from a crime scene while Elizabeth had stood, incredulous, behind the counter as I left her there with no explanation.

I couldn't tell her first, even though I knew she had to know the tests were positive based on my mad dash out her door. Cade had to be the first one I spoke the words out loud to.

"I'm pregnant", had been on repeat in my brain on a loop ever since this morning. I'd spent forever getting ready for tonight, twisting side to side in my full-length mirror searching for any physical sign that it was real, but of course, it was way too early for that.

"Oooh! Busted! You're not drinking tonight," she whispered. "Tell me I'm the first to know." She swiped the martini glass out of my hand, surreptitiously chugged the contents, and replaced it all in the span of approximately thirty seconds. "I got you. Your secret is safe with me."

"Thanks." I grinned at her. "And yes, you're technically the first. I'm telling Cade tonight when he gets home. He's been crazy busy at work all day. This is the kind of news one needs to deliver in person, you know?" Cade was the chief of the Sweetbriar police department. He spent his days keeping the town safe and his nights making me the happiest woman in the world.

"Oh, totally." She mimed zipping her lips. "I will not say a single word. I swear."

"You're good people, Elizabeth. I appreciate you."

"You would not believe the secrets I have stored up in

this brain of mine. People buy very telling combinations of random shit in a convenience store. Like a stack of pregnancy tests and a flight of Hot Pockets, for example..."

I let out a laugh. "I can only imagine."

"Speaking of that—*imagining*—how about you imagine a guest spot for me in your next book?" Her eyes twinkled into mine. "Can I help solve the murder? Or even better! Kill me off."

"You got it. Maybe some Stop-and-Go carnage? A murder in the chip aisle, or death by a poisoned Hot Pocket, perhaps?"

"I love all of that. I'll adore anything you write. I just want to be immortalized in one of your stories." We locked eyes. "I've decided. Kill me, Charli. Make it gory—"

We turned when Violet clinked a fork against her glass to get everyone's attention. "Let's raise our glasses and toast to our own Keli Marlowe's latest book."

The room broke out in cheers and congratulations, and as usual, I turned bright red with embarrassment. I lifted my empty glass and tossed a grin to Elizabeth.

"Congratulations, Charli," she murmured. "I'm thrilled for you. For the book baby and the baby baby."

"My next story will be extra gory. Just for you."

Soon enough, Gwen, my sisters-in-law, and all my Sweetbriar friends surrounded me, and I signed books, and I gave hugs as we chatted about stories and life. I could not be happier to finally be back home, where I belonged.

I was so lucky to have been able to create the life I'd always dreamed of and even luckier that I got to reclaim the one I had to leave behind to do it.

I couldn't wait to tell Cade he was going to be a father.

Dreams really could come true if you believed in yourself.

Baby, Baby

Cade

"Charli baby, I'm home." Exhausted, I stumbled through the front door of our cabin. All I wanted was to crawl into bed with my gorgeous wife and crash into a comatose oblivion for a few hours.

"I'm in the kitchen," she called.

Sometimes I still couldn't believe she was back, that we'd been married for almost a year. I had never been happier in my life.

I kicked off my boots and crossed the living room to get to her. I needed her in my arms again. Even a day away was sometimes too much to bear. I'd spent so many years without her. Having her back was like living inside of a dream I still couldn't quite believe was real.

I entered the kitchen to find her behind the counter pouring two glasses of sparkling cider into the glasses she only brought out on special occasions. "What's happening?" I pulled her against me, wrapping her in my arms to bury my face in her sweet-smelling neck. "I missed you."

"I missed you too, Cade. I love you so much."

"I love you too. What are we celebrating? The new book? I'm sorry I missed your party, sweetheart."

"It's okay. I got your roses, all three dozen of them." She gestured to the vases distributed around the house. "They're gorgeous. Thank you."

"Of course." I dropped a kiss to her upturned lips, running my hands into her hair, pulling her closer, letting myself get lost in her...

She pulled away, breathless and smiling. "I have something to show you first, Cade."

With a shake of my head, I pulled her back and kissed her again. "I don't need anything but you right now," I murmured against her lips. "Can it wait? I need you. Right now. You're so fucking beautiful, Charlotte. I'll never get enough." I let my hands drift down her back and over her luscious ass to lift her behind the thighs. Giving a little hop, she wrapped her legs around my waist as I kissed her deep.

Winding her arms around my neck, we melted into each other as I walked us down the hall to our bedroom.

"Wait! You got me all worked up, and this is important. Put me down so I can think straight. I promise it will be worth it."

I set her down. "Show me." My heart pounded in my ears, and I was hard as a rock, but I nodded at her to show me whatever it was that was more important than getting into bed and losing ourselves in each other.

She reached for my hand and led me back into the kitchen. "Remember after prom?"

I chuckled. "Yeah, I remember. Let's go back to bed and reenact it."

"After that, silly. Remember what we talked about?"

My mind cleared as my eyes hit hers and an anticipatory shiver shot through me. "Charli."

"Yeah, Cade. We decided on two kids. Remember?"

"How could I forget? Are you saying..."

She grabbed a plastic bag from the counter and waved it at me. "I'm saying I missed my period and peed on ten pregnancy tests today and they were all positive. I'm saying you're going to be a dad."

"Charli baby. I—" I was wrong. *Now,* I had never been happier.

Tears filled my eyes. I couldn't even brush them away; they came so fast. My heart was bursting with love. Filled to the brim with all the ways I could take care of her, and of our child. Nothing meant more to me than making sure she never regretted, not for one second, coming back home to Sweetbriar.

We stood there in the middle of the kitchen, staring at each other. Me, still in shock, jaw dropped, and her, with a plastic bag full of pregnancy tests in her hand, wearing an expression full of uncertainty on her face.

"Are you okay?" She finally said. "Is this—? Um, say something, Cade. Please."

"I fucking love you," I blurted.

A relieved giggle escaped as her body relaxed and the bag dropped to the floor. "I've never felt like this before,

Cade, even the first time around with you. I never dreamt it was possible to feel this content. And I'm a dreamer for a living, you know. My god, how I love you."

I knelt and kissed her stomach. "Hey in there, baby, it's your dad..." I pressed my cheek against her warmth and nuzzled close as I choked up from the overwhelming emotions flooding through me. "You're going to let me spoil the two of you rotten," I informed her as she ran her hands into my hair. "No arguments."

I squeezed her tight around her hips as she let out a laugh. "That sounds like heaven to me. As long as I get to do the same for you."

"You already have." I looked up, with my chin resting against her and her hands caressing my face, to brush my tears away. "I'm living my dream now. You were the only thing that was missing in my life and you're here again. Now that we're having a baby, I have everything. We're making a family, Charli."

"You gave me the world again, Cade. I didn't think it was possible to have it all. But look at us. We're so lucky. Take me back to bed."

"Anything you want." I stood and swept her into my arms to carry her back to our room.

Join Cade and Charlotte on their honeymoon! Scan the code to read the exclusive bonus scene!

About the Author

Nora Everly is a lifelong bookworm. She started reading the good stuff once she grew tall enough to sneak the romance novels off the top of her mother's bookshelf and it has been non-stop ever since.

Once upon a time she was a substitute teacher and an educational assistant. Now she's a writer and stay at home mom to two small humans and one fat cat.

Nora lives in the Pacific Northwest with her family and her overactive imagination.

Find her at noraeverly.com
Get all the Nora News!

Also by Nora Everly

The Sweetbriar Mountain Series:

In My Heart

Heart Words

From the Heart

Heart to Heart

Change of Heart

Honeybrook Hollow:

Next to You

Make You Mine

By Your Side

Sweetbriar Short Stories:

Holiday Hearts

Conversation Hearts

Let It Snow

The Cozy Creek Collection:

Fall at Once

From Smartypants Romance:

Oh Brother!

Crime and Periodicals

Carpentry and Cocktails

Hotshot and Hospitality

Architecture and Artistry

Teachers' Lounge

Passing Notes

Star Crossed Lovers:

(*As Piper Everly, co-written with Piper Sheldon*):
<u>Midnight Clear</u>

Get exclusive sneak peeks of upcoming releases through Nora's newsletter and Facebook group, The Everly Afters.